NOTES
FROM THE
TRAUMA PARTY

MICHAEL KEEN

TAILWINDS PRESS

Tailwinds Press
P.O. Box 2283, Radio City Station
New York, NY 10101-2283
www.tailwindspress.com

Published in the United States of America
ISBN: 979-8-9853124-6-1
1st ed. 2023

NOTES
FROM THE
TRAUMA PARTY

Every now is a vision of belief

                              - Denis Johnson

If I had to do the whole thing over again
I wouldn't

                              - John Berryman

I conduct weekly therapy with a client of mine, Bob, that I'm fairly certain is planning to kill me. He may not succeed in killing me but he's at least going to try or so my mind tells me given my last session with the man. During that session Bob was wild-eyed and tangential which is to say that his presence made it clear that something was very deeply wrong. And yes assuredly there are reasons to be concerned the most notable being that when Bob was last visibly psychotic he stabbed his cat twenty times in front of his wife and children. Based on what I've read of his intake and conversations I've had with his parole officer Bob did this because he thought his last therapist was cuckolding him and conspiring to kill him. Bob's murder of the cat was thus both retaliatory and protective which is to say that Bob became violent because he felt like he'd been cornered. He felt like he'd been cornered and betrayed. This worries me because it means he has a history of paranoia in relation to mental health professionals, a fact that lends credence to the idea that he thinks I'm a threat that needs to be eliminated. All of which means that there's a non-trivial possibility that Bob is going to shoot me or stab me or etc. I'm sufficiently concerned in fact that I feel the need to ask my supervisor, Monique, to meet with Bob on the morning of our next appointment. She agrees to meet him in the lobby and to briefly assess him and intends to explain my tardiness by saying I'm busy with another client. I'm in the bullpen at present waiting for Monique to return and while I wait I ruefully consider the possibility that I've sent Monique to her death. I breathe a sigh of relief when I see her reenter the bullpen and before I can ask her how Bob is doing she shrugs her shoulders and says that Bob was a no-show. There's a sinking feeling in my chest but I push my awareness of this away though of course I'll only recognize my denial for what it is in the future when I'm reexamining this moment. After calling Bob—who doesn't answer—I call Bob's emergency contact, his sister, who promptly informs me that Bob committed suicide several days before. Upon hearing this my world suddenly becomes very small and my only concern is not crying while on the phone with his sister. There's stupefaction in her voice whether from shock or grief or both I don't know but I do know that she thanks me for the work I did with Bob. Once the phone call is over I inform Monique that Bob killed himself and I take a break by walking around the building and staring at some flowers I don't know the name of. I cry at some point but I'm not sure of exactly when, I just know my mind repeatedly tells itself, "Don't let other people see you cry." Days and weeks later and it's like I'm not in my body not even when I shower and I alternate the water between cold and hot. Besides the feeling of guilt that hovers above me like some hideous and amorphous cloud what's most distressing during this period is the presence of intrusive images. At some point early on I heard that Bob's method of suicide was hanging and it's precisely this image—of Bob's body dangling from a rope—that I can't shake myself free of. The intrusive images last more than a month until one day I happen to talk to Bob's PO and learn that in fact Bob didn't hang himself at all. Apparently the means by which he killed himself involved a grocery bag taped around his head and a hose connected to a helium tank going into the bag. In all likelihood then Bob's final moments were painless though the elaborateness of the suicide mechanism still strikes me as unnerving. There are so many details I'm consumed with like the amount of tape he used to affix the bag to his head or the bag's provenance by which I mean did it come from Walmart, Safeway, or QFC? Or the sound of the tank. Was that the final sense datum Bob experienced? The dull hiss of the helium tank that supplied the oblivion-granting gas? These images supplant the old image of Bob's gently swinging and dangling body, an image embedded in my mind I think from the character of Brooks in the movie *The Shawshank Redemption*. In any case after I learn about the grocery bag and the helium tank I feel more than mildly ridiculous as I've been envisioning Bob's dead body in a way that was completely inaccurate. Verisimilitude is important or so I think in the aftermath of Bob's death by which I mean I view it as vital that I accurately perceive the man's corpse in my mind's eye. However most unnerving by far is what happens when I type Bob's name into Google and stumble upon an obituary that has details for a planned memorial. Should I go to the memorial? Does it make me a bad clinician if I don't? But if I did wouldn't it transgress a healthy boundary between my personal and professional lives? These questions are haunting and I don't know the right answer to any of them nor do I know them now, thirteen revolutions around the sun later. Thirteen years. Where does the time really go? And how is it possible that time can heal a psychic wound that was once utterly crippling? Does time actually heal all wounds? Of course not, Michael. Of course not. But in this case it did and Bob's death didn't even leave a scar. I can't even remember what Bob looks like to be honest. All I remember are his red-rimmed eyes when we said goodbye. His red-rimmed eyes, his trembling hands, and his scared shitless, what-do-I-do-now quavering voice.

"Welcome back!" my dealer says even though he's tearing up less than a minute later, in this case because I ghosted him nine months ago when I got sober. I marvel at the sequence of events, wondering if it's normal to perform emotional labor for the man who sells you drugs, and as I hear the pain in his voice I realize I'm going to have to lie. "I thought we were friends," he says. "Friends don't just leave each other, bro." Zeke shields his face as he says this but I know it's distorted with grief and it then occurs to me how hard it must be for cocaine dealers to have such high customer turnover. People moving on to other dealers. People going to rehab. People finding God. Any gram a person buys having the potential to be their last. I feel an upwelling of compassion for the man, realizing how lonely Zeke must feel, but this upwelling is short-lived as my primary objective is putting powder up my nose. I consider my immediate options—do I say I was depressed? In financial hardship? That I started and ended a relationship in the last nine months?—but all that's clear to me is that I can't confess the truth. If I do I risk not doing drugs as the truth would invariably cause Zeke to feel tremendous guilt or if not guilt then at least it would give him pause about enabling the relapse of an addict. Or maybe not. I don't know. Maybe Zeke knows his destiny is to orchestrate my fall from grace. And maybe that's as it should be. Maybe falling from grace is what I was put on earth to do.

It's morning and the air is still and I'm making a ditch for rainwater runoff when I take a break and lean my body against the shovel. I'm 18 years old and I've spent the last six months at a Buddhist monastery, in fact that's where I'm at, in the San Jacinto Mountains at a place called Zen Mountain Center. I'm leaving the monastery in a number of days and in three months I'll start college which I'm excited about so much so that it feels basically unreal. That's at the center of this moment it's why I still resonate with it decades later, it's because of the excitement I feel about the future as I lean against the shovel. I feel the sun streaming and I hear the birds chirping and the air smells of smoke from a controlled brush-fire being burned on the grounds. It all just feels so unbelievably expansive. Like everything is beginning. Like everything in my life is only now beginning. "Remember this," I say and it's like I'm talking to myself through the veil of time which of course I am in a sense I'm in dialogue with you the sad supine old man presently yielding up his final breath. You're not really alone old man though of course yes you also are alone as besides death being marooned inside our skulls is our sole inheritance as sentient beings. But no not now this isn't the time for abstractions I see no wisdom as I lean against the shovel and gape out at that blue cloudless never-ending sky. I'm too young to have wisdom and even if I did what good would it do me I'd still end my life looking back longingly to a place I no longer am. In the world but not of it as the ancient story goes and in my case it's true I've spent my whole life learning how to become fog. And it's working, it is, in fact one day I'll become fog completely for all I know I already have and these words are all that's left of the sun, the birds, the smoke, and that cloudless never-ending sky.

It's my second semester at Berkeley and my acne's gotten bad, to such a degree in fact that I'm now cripplingly self-conscious. I look in the mirror for hours each day despising who and what I see and as I do so I feel grotesque and unloved and disgusting. I pop pimples and apply creams that are largely if not entirely ineffective and even on those occasions they are effective they invariably leave me looking like a burn victim with flaky skin. One of the main medications, benzoyl peroxide, also has the unfortunate side effect of bleaching clothes which means that over the course of my college years I ruin hundreds if not thousands of dollars' worth of clothing. At the height of my skin-fixation I walk to various restrooms across campus in order to evaluate my skin in different mirrors. I want the unvarnished truth and feel like aggregating data from mirrors will provide that and also feel that if I know the truth then I can finally accept it. Or so I tell myself as I examine my skin in various buildings' restrooms' mirrors only to start washing my hands whenever anyone else enters the room. My skin-fixation is shameful and I don't want other people to know the truth by which I mean it's important to me that people think I don't care about my blemishes. Beauty's only skin deep or so the prevailing wisdom goes which is to say that an obsession with surface suggests I'm a superficial person. I want to be a person of substance and depth and that seems incompatible with the life I'm currently living, defined as it is by fifteen minutes in the law building restroom, ten minutes in the math building, etc. Eventually I meet with my dermatologist and break down in tears during the meeting and because I'm at the end of my rope I ask him if I can start Accutane. The latter's an oral retinoid that sometimes has severe side effects most notably psychiatric side effects that can include suicidal ideation. However by this point in my psychiatric journey I'm already on Wellbutrin and Lexapro which is to say that the psych meds in my system will likely inure me against psychiatric problems. Plus even if they didn't the fact is that acne is making me so anxious and depressed that any suicidality induced by Accutane would be identical to the life I'm currently living. Soon thereafter I start Accutane which among other things reduces the size of the sebaceous glands and sure enough I have to start moisturizing in order to compensate for my now perpetually dry skin. I gain confidence and start to peacock and by the end of five months my skin is basically completely normal by which I mean that now I only get the occasional minor blemish. I no longer feel strange or exceptional which as it turns out is exactly what I want I want to turn my mind off and function as just another member of the herd. Is this healthy? A sign of weakness? I don't know nor in reality can I say I really care. I just want to make it out of this thing alive until it's my time to no longer be alive.

I'm in Portland and I'm speeding as I've probably done a gram in under 90 minutes and the man I'm with, Nick, is poised to tell me something momentous. I know this because he says this, because he says, "I have something to tell you that I've never told anybody," and in my amped-up state I wonder what it could be. The air feels heavy and grave and I suspect he's going to tell me something really heinous maybe that he's raped someone or something of that nature. A part of me wants to assert a boundary, to tell him that I'm not capable of carrying another weighty psychic burden, especially given my recent breakup with my fiancée and my obvious problems with bipolar and addiction. Nevertheless I'm high and so the larger part of me feels invulnerable to negative energy which means that I encourage this man to clear his obviously enormously laden conscience. In fact I'm so busy trying to reassure the man in front of me, to make him feel comfortable and safe, that it takes me time to process it when he says that he masturbates to child pornography. I then say nothing as he manically rambles and explains to me why he's selected me as the person to tell, a selection he made evidently because of what I said earlier about people attracted to children. I said, "As long as he doesn't act on it, a pedophile is worthy of pity. No one would choose to be attracted to a child." As he quotes me to myself I recall the context of the quote which involved me talking about one of my social work jobs where I worked with a number of sex offenders. Obviously I said much more than this including that raping a child is maybe the worst thing a person can do and that people have to be held accountable for their crimes. I remind the man of that and soon thereafter he begins to weep and even more he begins repeating a question like a mantra. "Do you think I'm evil?" he asks over and over again, and at that moment it occurs to me that I have an extraordinary degree of power. I can exacerbate his shame and self-loathing by emphasizing the monstrosity of what he's done but my gut tells me that this isn't what's required most by the moment. Yes he's done evil and yes in viewing child pornography he's complicit in the rape of children but my goal isn't to be judge, jury, and executioner. I can't justify my reaction but one of my first thoughts is that Nick wouldn't do well in prison, a thought given legitimacy when he says he'd hang himself if he had to do time. I ask him if he's taking precautions to not get caught and he assures me that he is and after loathing myself for being more concerned about his safety than the safety of the children being abused I reflect on the appropriate course of action. As I do so I blow my nose and observe an alarming quantity of blood in the paper towel but by this stage in my cocaine use I'm not fazed by blood at all. I'm then systematic in what I say, exploring how he could stop his consumption of child pornography, including masturbating to other genres, seeking out a professional, etc. However the man shakes his head sadly, obviously crestfallen by my advice, as nothing I say seems like it will be effective. I say, "You're not evil, but this action is evil. You have to promise me that you're going to stop doing this." He then looks at the floor or maybe his hands, somewhere away from me in any event, and he admits to me that that isn't a promise he can make. Thus do we arrive at a standstill because the man refuses to change his hideous behavior and I for a litany of reasons including lack of evidence and fear of reprisal refuse to report him to the police. What's particularly grotesque is near the end of our conversation when he attempts to normalize his behavior and place it on a continuum with other men. He says, "Most men are attracted to 18-year-olds. So why is 16 or 17 all that strange?" I attempt to reason with the man again, to make it clear that it's wrong to consume images of statutory rape, but there's no reaching the man he's already gone. "Thanks for not judging me," the man says though I do obviously judge him, if not existentially then at least on the level of behavior. I ask myself, "What does it say about me that someone feels comfortable confessing to me that they look at child pornography?" I'm not sure but I'm guessing it means I'm too morally permissive. The conversation peters out and both of us know the pocket of intensity is over and that also in all likelihood the man will never make his confession to anyone again. I pity the man pity and hate him as he's made me complicit in his complicity and as a victim of child rape I don't appreciate being asked to be complicit in what he's done. Nevertheless what could he do but confess for all I know it may have even been healing he wept after all not that that necessarily means any healing occurred. All I know is that during the conversation 75 minutes quickly passed and throughout that period I haven't thought about doing cocaine not even once. That's a miracle if there ever was one although yes I now carry the weight of another man doing unspeakable things and yes I feel like some sort of Judas who's betrayed my fellow victims of child rape. But I don't know what can I do I'm not going to send the man to prison maybe most people would die on this hill but to me there are no hills it's all flatland as far as the eye can see and we're all being crucified in our own idiosyncratic way. Or at least that's what I tell myself as I cut myself a line which I deserve I think I deserve a respite from this beautiful sad pathetic fucking world.

My first serious girlfriend, Zoe, fell in love with me three months into our relationship, a fact she announced over the phone knowing full well I wasn't going to reciprocate. And she was right. I didn't reciprocate. I did effusively thank her—for her courage, her kindness, her tenderness, honesty, and vulnerability—but conspicuously I said nothing about also being in love with her. Zoe knew her actions would create a rift and in fact they have created a rift, one we both have attempted to approach with tolerance and patience in the weeks that have followed. The rift nevertheless is there and over time I can feel Zoe start to emotionally pull away, a self-protective mechanism that is understandable albeit extremely sad to witness. Finally one night after class I arrive at her apartment and see from her demeanor that the entire issue has come to a head. She'd made dinner for herself earlier and has already eaten but she offers me the leftover steak that she cooked. As I eat she says nothing and her eyes dart around the kitchen, seemingly terrified of interrogating me and in so doing our relationship. I eat the steak quickly as it's clear that Zoe wants to talk and that furthermore she wants to do the talking in her bedroom. Zoe's sensitive and emotional and we both know that she's liable to get upset, particularly given the conversation we both know we're going to have. Plus her roommate is home which poses the risk of a conversation in the kitchen being disrupted, an eventuality that's undesirable especially if Zoe starts to cry. So I finish the steak and we move to the bedroom and while I stand Zoe sits on her bed, at which point she tenderly enfolds one hand in the other. She's attempting to compose herself, to find some place of peace within the vast chaos of her heart, and eventually she closes her eyes, takes a deep breath, and begins. Zoe then proceeds to unload and speaks for over ten minutes, divulging every last bit of her thought process over the last two months. There's nuance to her thinking but the bones of it are simple resting as it does on the idea that she can't be in a relationship where there's no possibility of love being mutually felt. Eventually the peregrinations stop and she arrives at her central purpose which simply put is to ask me whether I think there's any possibility that I can love her. Her reason for asking as she explains is that though she's undeniably in love with me she can't justify remaining in our relationship if there's no way that I can love her. To do so would be masochistic and painful and abject and pathetic and though she feels weak and vulnerable right now she won't allow herself to do so. "So what do you think?" she asks. "Is there any way that you could love me?" My instinctual gut-level response is to say that I can't and as Zoe wrings her hands I consider how I'm going to break the news. The basic tack I plan on using is to say that I'm never going to love anyone, either because love is a myth created by Hallmark or because I'm elementally defective. I'm vacillating between the two strategies and am poised to start speaking when suddenly it occurs to me that I have a way out. That is to say Zoe has given me the means by which I can avoid saying something potentially extraordinarily hurtful. I can in other words forestall our inevitable breakup by telling her that I don't know for sure. After all it is possible—at least on some vague theoretical level—that I could fall in love with Zoe at some point in the future. Love could descend like an angel, or maybe rain, or etc., and for all I know my entire approach to and understanding of love would be completely transfigured. This then is what I tell her. That I find it unlikely I'll fall in love but that it is possible in the way that improbable events sometimes come to pass. Zoe vigorously nods as if I've confirmed what she privately suspected and she then begins to rock back and forth on the bed as she semi-violently wrings her hands. The moment feels precious and private and I feel voyeuristic observing what she's doing, as her level of vulnerability is so extreme that it feels intolerable to witness. Zoe starts sobbing at this point and in between her sobs she starts to groan, groaning, "As long as there's a chance! As long as there's a chance! I can forgive myself for staying with you!" She just keeps saying that to herself, as if she's hypnotized somehow, like it's a mantra. The sum total of which tableau leaves me absolutely stunned. Because she's letting it all hang out, her love for me her desperation her neediness. She's just so vulnerable right now that I can't even process it. All of which is to say: I don't know what it is that does it. If it's that she's so unbelievably vulnerable, or the fact that I stop putting pressure on myself, or what. All I can say is that regardless of how awkward the whole thing sounds, that's it. That's the moment. That's the moment I first fall in love. The moment I move past myself and see how beautiful it is to live as one of the condemned.

"We're gonna start a podcast, bro," says the man slumped over on the beanbag chair and I know in his heart the bastard believes it. I vigorously nod after he makes the comment but my attention is riveted on the tray being passed around, a tray that has enough lines on it to accommodate all six customers in the room. He says, "We're vibing, man. Really connecting. Shit like this doesn't happen every single day. You know what I mean by that, right?" I again nod but say nothing, still engrossed by the spectacle of the tray being passed around, and I'm dimly aware that my jaw is jutting about. "Hey," the man says, his tone perched somewhere between sadness and accusation. "You agree that we're vibing, don't you, bro?" I then accept the tray—it's handed to me by an eighteen-year-old girl with a septum piercing—and lift up my finger to buy time before responding. I place the dollar bill in my nose and snort the largest of the remaining lines and reflexively cough before turning to my wounded friend. I then look him in the eyes, his eyes that are somehow both vacant and tinged with light, and say, "Dude, I've never vibed with anyone so hard in my life."

I'm seated on one of the beanbag chairs and I'm talking with a man and his wife, each of whom is intermittently taking hits off a crack pipe. "We live with her mom," the man says. "Just moved to Seattle a month and a half ago. Trying to find jobs, and trying to not get on her mom's nerves." The man's eyes are lifeless and shark-like. His wife absently nods. As she takes another hit I ask them how they became acquainted with Zeke. "My mom buys from Zeke," the woman says, this though the woman looks like she's 35, which would mean a 50-to-60-year-old woman coordinated for her daughter to meet a crack dealer. I ask the two what crack is like, intrigued by the experiential differences between cocaine and crack, and the woman offers the boilerplate I've heard a thousand times before. Namely that crack is shorter and more intense, a description that's vague but still piques my interest, and part of me hopes the couple will offer me a chance to partake. But they don't and soon leave Zeke's at which point I'm left with the usual motley crew by which I mean Chris, Courtney, and the other disciples, of light or darkness I'll never know.

I'm twelve and at my house and with my childhood friend, Abe, and the two of us are watching a video my father rented, *Traces of Death*. All manner of butchery is depicted in the film, some of which is real and some isn't, but among the grisly tableaux is footage of a man, R. Budd Dwyer, shooting himself in the mouth at a press conference. Unlike some of the other material in the film and unlike other horror-mockumentaries I've seen there's no way this footage of Dwyer is staged. In other words there was a man who really did call a press conference and did shoot himself in the mouth and who then really did have blood hemorrhage out of his nose. My sensation when watching the footage is unlike any other sensation I can ever recall, the closest analogue being an experience which occurred when I was in second grade. The catalyst for this latter experience was pathetically enough a Victoria's Secret catalogue, the images in which, when observed, I felt inexplicably drawn to. This feeling of being drawn to the images was magnetic, it was all-consuming, upending, etc., which is to say that my attraction was sufficiently overwhelming that I lost whatever bearings I had. So overwhelmed in fact was I at that moment, so consumed was I by the talismanic power of these near-naked women, that I did what had to be done to absorb their power: I tore out the images of three or four of the women from the catalogue and stuffed the images in my underwear, at which point I talked to my parents, ate food, and watched TV for an hour. Throughout these latter activities my attention was obviously totally divided which is to say that my essential energy was focused on the feeling of transgression. I was doing ostensibly normal things but I was doing them while delectating in an unknown feeling, a feeling that at that age was so unknown that I couldn't parse it as good or bad. It simply was, and was overwhelming, and was so powerful that I could scarcely endure the force of my desire which is another way of saying that I was immersing myself in something that for all I knew was evil and wrong. As it turned out this feeling wasn't wrong but was in fact simply the proto-sexual impulse but nevertheless for a period the possibility existed that I was willfully transgressing a norm and engaging in behavior that was evil. This delectation in transgression also describes the feeling I encountered when seeing R. Budd Dwyer's suicide, at least insofar as I felt helplessly riveted by something that by all appearances was wrong. Of course the difference between the two was that the sight of Dwyer's hemorrhaging blood and glassy eyes actually *was* deeply corrosive which is to say that unlike the underwear incident viewing Dwyer's suicide was morally and existentially wrong. The scene wasn't meant for human consumption, certainly not the consumption of a child, and it forced me to attempt to reconcile the irreconcilable. What I mean by irreconcilable is that my childish mentality held that life was inherently meaningful and this naïve belief in meaning couldn't be squared with Dwyer's corpse slumped over on the ground. The superficial description and analysis would be to say that there's a pornographic quality to the Dwyer footage at least insofar as it elicits a frisson of negative energy. However I think it's important to say that this analysis is fundamentally flawed and to my mind that's precisely because the Dwyer footage doesn't function in any way to get me off. In fact as bizarre as it sounds—and this connects back to the need to reconcile the irreconcilable—I think the Dwyer footage elicits a kind of sublimated religious impulse. "If life is beautiful and redemptive, where's the redemption in this hideous act?" Though I don't know how to express this question at the time it is the fundamental question I'm confronting and the image of the hemorrhaging blood haunts me in part because I can't find an answer that satisfies me. (This because there is no answer). Sadly the Dwyer footage isn't the end. Over the many years that follow I'll view footage of all manner of suicides and murders. I view many of these videos while I'm in college once I discover the website rotten.com, and later when rotten becomes defunct similar material is on the website ogrish.com. Hangings, death by firearms, leaps from buildings, etc. The brutal images exist like a bloody mist before my mind's eye. From 22 to 30 I minimally engage with this world, only to reenter it when ISIS begins releasing videos of executions. I see one video for instance where a man is shot in the head at close range with a gun using exploding ammunition. The effect of the blast is that half of the man's head is removed, leaving only a grotesque bulbous mass that is a nightmarish shade of pink. "This isn't meant to be seen," I say as I close the window that has the ISIS video, but the regrettable fact is that I have seen these videos and I'll never unsee them. I may not think of them every moment. I may not be consumed by their irredeemable grotesquerie. But at any moment in time I can direct you to some monstrous piece of footage and offer irrefutable proof that there's no meaning here and there never ever was.

"You meet a bunch of these criteria. I think you're clinically depressed. And I think you should try antidepressants." Tony's pointing at a piece of paper when he says this and his hands are mildly shaking, the latter being an indication of how vulnerable he is. He's my best friend at this time of my life and I live with his family in Bellingham, Washington, as for various reasons I've elected not to live with my own family in Puyallup for my senior year of high school. I've been unable to focus this whole year and my GPA has dipped from a 4.0 to a 2.5, this because of a catastrophic drug experience I had at the end of my junior year. During that experience—which was precipitated by the psychedelic compound found in Hawaiian baby woodrose seeds—I felt like a valve in my brain opened that has never fully closed. During the height of the drug experience I scratched my legs as I sat on the porch of my house and while I did so I had a vision of being committed to a mental institution. In the vision my parents were wringing their hands and lamenting how much potential I'd had as a child and how my decision to do drugs had instantly robbed me of that potential. The drug of course wore off eventually as drugs are wont to do but nevertheless this whole year I've felt susceptible to panic attacks and depression. One reason I elected to leave my family was because I blamed my father for the experience, as he recommended I take psychedelics and even used his credit card to purchase the seeds for me online. In the aftermath of my psychic meltdown I was looking for someone or something to blame and fair or not my father made a very convenient scapegoat. At his hands I experienced years of childhood abuse which involved him endlessly screaming at me, my mom, my sister, and the world at large, so much screaming in fact that it now seems cartoonish. Two decades later and he still calls my mother a cunt to her face countless times per day and on several occasions has even in all seriousness threatened to murder me. On one particularly notable occasion he carried a hammer around the house and said he was going to bash my head in that night while I was sleeping. He's also unbelievably racist, most notably toward black people, black culture, and all things Arab, to such a degree in fact that I once found a folder on his computer entitled "Why All Arabs Must Die." But enough about my father it seems like that's all I ever talk about now as an adult, my father, my rape as a child, and my almost fatal drug addiction. The point is that in the aftermath of the drug experience I was mentally adrift and clearly suffering, I was suffering and Tony is the only friend who respected me enough to tell me what he thought. He was strong enough to risk my wrath, to risk me excoriating him for his arrogance and impudence and etc., and twenty years on I should tell him how much his trembling hands meant to me, how to me they symbolize sacrifice, friendship, and love. I should tell him but I won't as I'm a coward who can only tolerate vulnerability when I encounter it in a book or a film and this isn't either of those it's just me and a friend together at a table eating and me unable to say what I really want to say. Except here.

I'm drunk and it's late and I'm in a convenience store in a city outside Osaka when two Yakuza members ask me if I want to go on a joyride. I'm in Japan to teach English and have spent the bulk of the night carousing and am only in the convenience store at all because I need to hydrate before bed. And yet still nevertheless despite my incredibly drunken state there's no doubt whatsoever that the men before me are Yakuza. They're arrogant and contemptuous and seem to have no interest in being polite and the impression I have is that they're only talking to me out of a vague sense of curiosity. Of course the most important piece of data is that both men are covered in tattoos and as any Japanese person will tell you only Yakuza members have tattoos in this country. All of this I'm aware of—the tattoos, the brusque demeanor, the contemptuous curl of their lips—and yet inexplicably I agree to get in their vehicle. Like me the men are drunk and like me they're shocked by what I've agreed to but soon one of the men puts his arm across my shoulders. In Japanese he says, "We're going to party, gaijin!" and we walk arm-in-arm to the front of the store as the other Yakuza member buys beer for the three of us. I feel myself nodding and laughing, not having any real idea why, presumably just because the man touching me is extremely enthusiastic about my presence. It's only as I'm leaving the store, specifically when I see the concern in the eyes of the other people present, that I realize I've made a rash and unwise decision. Soon I've entered the van's back seat and I've closed its sliding door at which point the driver lights a joint, an action that deeply unnerves me. Marijuana is hard to come by in Japan, one reason for which being that the consequences of possession are severe, the knowledge of which fact makes me reluctant to partake. We then begin driving around the city, Kishiwada, and after the two Yakuza members have had their fill of mj the one in the passenger seat offers the joint to me. I gently decline the offer several times which clearly irritates the Yakuza members, a fact I gather from the increasingly aggressive tone of the driver's voice. At this point the non-driving Yakuza member joins me in the back of the van and begins interrogating me about what I'm doing in his country. Neither Yakuza member speaks English or at least they make no concessions to me by attempting to speak it which means that I'm forced to communicate solely in Japanese while knee-deep in a brownout. What makes matters worse is that the men aren't making any other accommodations either, accommodations that might include speaking slowly, with simple diction, etc. In fact if anything the Yakuza members are making it impossible for me to understand them, given for example the rate at which they're speaking and the slang that they're using. Now the driver pulls up in front of a building where a dolled-up woman is waiting and before I can even ask who she is we're driving on and she's in the passenger seat. Is she a sex worker? The girlfriend of one of the men? I don't know and my suspicion is that I never will, as the Yakuza members clearly have no interest in making an introduction between me and the woman. At this point I begin to panic because the Yakuza member in the back of the van begins to slap me, first lightly but then with an increasing amount of force. He laughs whenever he does so, calling me baka and gaijin over and over again, and my only concern right now is how I can extricate myself from the vehicle. The (possible) sex worker at this point turns around and speaks to the Yakuza member crouched next to me in the back, and though she's speaking quickly I piece together that she's advising them to get rid of me. Hearing this terrifies me because it's unclear to me whether she's instructing them to murder me and hide my body or what and meanwhile the one Yakuza member is continuing to slap me in the face. Eventually he shrugs his shoulders and yells something to the driver, the latter of whom pulls over immediately and barks angrily at me. I look into the eyes of the sex worker and glean nothing and look at the Yakuza member in the back and glean nothing and reluctantly but necessarily say wakarimasen one final time. The man in the back then lunges toward me which makes me think he's about to stab me but as it turns out he's only opening the van's sliding door. This same man then gestures at me to leave which I'm in the process of rapidly doing when I feel myself being literally kicked out of the vehicle. I hear the three vehicle occupants laugh and hear myself called baka one final time at which point they drive away and I pull myself up off of the ground. I'm close to my apartment which is borderline miraculous given the circumstances as the thugs obviously could have dropped me off anywhere they wanted to. Instead I'm here near my apartment which is to say my home away from home although if traveling has taught me anything it's that I have no home, no rest, no comfort, I have absolutely nothing.

The sun is shining and the wind whips past me and my legs feel like they're pedaling of their own accord as I chase after my friend, Nate, on my too-big bicycle, a hideous Huffy White Heat. It's summer and we're exploring and our travels take us to Wildwood elementary where we leave our bikes on the ground as we amble around the property. We hopscotch from topic to topic—Ren and Stimpy, our future professions, girls we have crushes on, etc.—and while we talk we see two older boys standing near the jungle gym. We're going to enter fifth grade soon and I peg the boys to be eighth graders at least although at my age anyone out of elementary school seems like they inhabit a different dimension. The older of the boys waves us over which is unnerving to both Nate and me, to such a degree on Nate's part in fact that he suggests we leave the elementary school right away. I'm afraid of the boys and skeptical but I feel the need to somehow prove myself, to prove to them and Nate and myself that I'm not a coward. I take the lead and Nate follows behind me until eventually the two of us reach the jungle gym at which point the two older boys acknowledge us with juts of the chin. At close range it's clear that the boys are not only older but lower-class, as their clothing is ratty and frayed and the two look as if they haven't attended to their personal hygiene. None of this occurs to me now—it's only in hindsight that I'll understand this—but what does occur to me is that the boys are tough and not to be fucked with in any way. "The slides are pretty fun," the younger kid says. "You should go down that one and check it out."

There are two slides as part of the jungle gym and the boys point at the shorter slide, the one that's closer to Nate, and it's only with reluctance that Nate climbs the ladder and goes down the slide. "Pretty good," the older one says. "But it's a lot more fun if you go down the slide with your eyes closed. You should try that with the other one. If you have the balls to, anyway." There's a menacing quality to what he's said but I'm intent on proving myself, on meeting the challenge. As I approach the ladder Nate looks at me worriedly and shakes his head. I ignore the rebuke he's given me and mindlessly climb the ladder to the top of the slide, the slide which points the opposite direction of the slide Nate went down. I firmly close my eyes entrusting my safety to some power greater than myself and as I begin to slide I'm confident that I'm going to be rewarded for what I'm doing. Namely with respect, both on the part of the boys and from Nate, but also from whatever invigilating presence is seeing me act bravely in the face of my fear. The experience of sliding is anti-climactic as the experience on a short slide invariably is and when I get to the bottom of the slide I open my eyes defiantly and stare at the older boys. They briefly return my stare and have a cryptic curl to their lips and I'm waiting for them to congratulate me when I notice the sensation of wetness on my legs and shorts. The older one then says, "You just slid into our piss, you fucking faggot!" at which point the two boys launch into hysterics, pointing at me and Nate while clapping each other on the back. Whether it's psychosomatic or not I suddenly feel my legs begin to itch, as if the boys' urine were some sort of acid eating away at my legs. Tears come to my eyes immediately and I raise myself off of the slide at which point Nate and

I run away toward our bikes. Nate says nothing—what can he say?—and as we ride away we hear the boys exclaim "faggot" a few more times, and during the bike ride home I basically dissociate from my body. True I register the wetness of my clothing and also the burning sensation on my legs and I observe the noxious odor of urine emanating from my body. But that's it. That's all I remember about the bike ride. At some point I return home and share the episode with my parents and they comfort me to the degree that they can. I then shower and put on clean clothing and watch *The Simpsons* while not watching *The Simpsons* and all I know is that splayed out on the couch newly clean I still feel utterly hollow. I feel hollow and humiliated and to this very day I feel like there's a wedge between me and my body, not that this wedge is largely attributable to the urine on the slide. No. Not at all. This is just a minor incident in the horror show of life. Just one of the many anecdotes I'm regaling strangers with at the cosmic trauma party.

At the ATM again and no I don't want to check my balance it's low but I can deal with that later. Yes I'll accept the surcharge and yes I understand the machine will only dispense twenties I don't care I just want the money in my hands. I type in 200 and soon the machine belches out my cash and for some reason the money feels greasy in my fingers. I can't afford what I'm doing I still have to pay rent oh well I'll just have to get more money from my mother. My mother. My sweet mother. My long-suffering, saintly mother. How many thousands of her dollars have I spent on cocaine? I make no effort to perform this calculation but instead take the receipt from the ATM and crumple it up before throwing it away. "I have to stop this soon," I mutter to myself as I begin the ten-minute walk to Zeke's. But not tonight. No, that's a conversation for another day.

Why does every nursing home I go to have a fish tank in its lobby? This is what I wonder as I sign in at a nursing home in Brooklyn and my gorge rises at the telltale reek of the facility. My nose detects bleach, urine, food, rubbing alcohol, and feces, which based on my time in hospice is representative as far as olfactory experiences go. I make my way through the facility until I reach the room of my patient, Albert, a man whose voice I've never heard despite having visited him weekly for a year. Albert's afflicted with late-stage dementia and is completely aphasic and what's horrifying is that he doesn't seem to recognize anyone around him. This includes his wife, Shelly, who visits him three times per week, this despite him being completely non-responsive in her presence. My supervisor, Kathleen, tells me that Shelly has a boyfriend outside of the facility which initially bothered me but now it doesn't whatsoever. What is Shelly supposed to do her husband is a living corpse after all, an inanimate object with pressure ulcers and a thousand-yard stare. I visit Albert on Fridays and when I do so I sit in a chair facing his bed though of course I could sit anywhere and it would make no difference at all. I luxuriate in the silence of his room, a silence that's only occasionally interrupted by the groaning of someone else in the facility. When I first met the man I used to periodically step into his line of vision, this so that I could gaze into his eyes. I naively believed that I could latch onto some morsel of humanity, that I could reach into the abyss and somehow drag the man out. In this I obviously failed as his illness had robbed him of every last remnant of identity or at least I thought this was the case after the few times I did so. This changed seven months ago when a nurse came into the room and asked me if I knew about Albert's past as a boxer. I informed the woman that I didn't at which point she told me Albert had had a long career, a fact that was only interesting to me insofar as it offered a potential explanation for Albert's dementia. The nurse then said, "Albert! Box!"—a command that produced a furrow in Albert's brow and that soon caused him to raise his fists and begin punching the air. "Jesus!" I said to myself, stupefied by the knowledge that Albert's spirit hadn't been 100% extinguished, a reality that sickened me because of its potential implications. Namely that Albert was aware of his abjection and actually deeply wanted to communicate with the outside world but because of the ravages of his illness could only do so in this one narrow pathetic way. Ever since that day I've been tempted to ask Albert to box when we're alone but I never have and I don't think that I will. What would be the point? Failing to communicate is painful and that's what I'd be doing I'd be asking Albert to try and inevitably fail to reach out to the larger world. Better to have never reached out at all. Or maybe not. Maybe the obverse is true. I just know being alone is painful enough without having to be reminded that you're alone.

One day I show up to school and my teacher, Mrs. Allen, is nowhere to be seen which on its own isn't in any way alarming. I'm in fifth grade by now and have had a substitute teacher on many occasions and so when I see the substitute, Mr. Bentham, in our classroom I think absolutely nothing of it. However there's a stiffness to his bearing, a formality I've never seen, which I think is strange given how relaxed Mr. Bentham has always appeared to be. He has a messy mop of hair and is recognizably a former hippie, as evidenced by his earthy energy and a tie of his depicting the cover of the Beatles record, *Sgt. Pepper's Lonely Hearts Club Band.* He seems grave and on edge, an observation that makes me distressed myself, as I've long become accustomed to the man's relaxed presence. This sense of distress substantially increases when right before the bell rings the principal and school counselor appear in our room. They too look distressed as if they are poised to deliver extremely bad news which as we soon learn is precisely what they're here to do. Evidently Mrs. Allen's husband has committed suicide, an action that we understand to be traumatic and catastrophic, though of course as fifth graders we—or at least I—have only a vague understanding of death. Nevertheless several members of my class begin to cry, a behavior I mimic though I'm uncertain of why, baffling as the entire situation is. "Why did he do what he did?" a classmate asks and the adults in the room all look at each other, baffled themselves at how to answer that question. The solemn nature of the moment suddenly recalls an experience I had in second grade, the experience that is of being told by my second-grade teacher, Mrs. Biven, that the class rabbit had died. When Mrs. Biven shared this information much of the class began to keen, to such a degree in fact that the present experience in fifth-grade feels subdued. I feel ashamed by the memory as I recall that I was more bothered by the death of the rabbit than I am by the death of Mrs. Allen's husband, a reaction that produces an upwelling of guilt on my part. Mainly however I feel confused and look to the adults for how to act, all of whom seem sad, confused, helpless, and alone. After school I'll learn more details from my mother, a fellow teacher and close friend of Mrs. Allen's, including that the latter's husband performed the suicide by jumping off the Tacoma-Narrows Bridge. My mother also says that according to the suicide note of Mrs. Allen's husband he was secretly addicted to cocaine and felt that there was no hope for recovery. Strangely it's this detail—that the man's addiction was a secret concealed even from his wife, Mrs. Allen—that I find to be almost unbearably sad. How lonely he must have felt! How lonely and fundamentally unseen! The other detail I can't escape is the fact that her husband jumped off a bridge. In me the image produces all manner of questions. How long was the drop to the water? Did the man die immediately upon impact? I imagine the man doing a swan dive but I'm sure that can't be correct. All of this swirls around my mind as I attend to the behavior of my classmates, none of whom seem to have a pure unmediated response. That is to say every one of my peers is looking around the room at everyone else, hoping that someone anyone will guide them in the feeling of vicarious grief. One week later I attend the memorial for Mrs. Allen's husband and in fact I'm the only student present from her class. I was reluctant to attend but my mother insisted it would mean a great deal to Mrs. Allen and so I sit in the pew next to my mother, father, and sister. Throughout the memorial my eyes are riveted on the back of Mrs. Allen's head, Mrs. Allen and her daughter, Melanie. I learn from my mother that Melanie's a year younger than I am which saddens me because it means I've known my father longer than she'll ever know hers. "Life isn't fair," I think as the memorial ends and Mrs. Allen files past me clutching the hand of her daughter. Her grief is so pure as to be obscene, as if to observe it is to stare at the sun, and decades later I'll still recall how Mrs. Allen's hands trembled with each wobbly step that she took. "Life isn't fair," I'll think again as Mrs. Allen finally exits the frame. Life isn't fair and all of us know it.

I'm at an AA meeting and a man I've never seen volunteers to share, a man who looks like a hipster and has tortoise-shell glasses. The man appears pretentious yes but his general bearing functions as a kind of counterpoint to this appearance, rooted as the bearing is in slowness and softness and consideration. After the man, Bryson, introduces himself he shares the story of how he arrived at AA, a story that begins with an addiction to heroin that was active as of four months ago. At that time Bryson had a close friend, Ben, whom he frequently used drugs with and that on one particular occasion Bryson texted in order to coordinate plans to do heroin. Imagine Bryson's surprise and horror when he received a text in reply to his that said Ben had died two nights before of a drug overdose. The sender was Ben's mother, a person in recovery herself, and after notifying Bryson of Ben's death she invited Bryson to an AA meeting that very night. Bryson has been a member of AA ever since, owing some large measure of his sobriety to his dead friend's mother, a woman he only came into contact with because of the overdose of Ben. I approach Bryson after the meeting, still stupefied by the power of his story, and in the coming months I'll think of his story often. That leads me to right now when on Capitol Hill I see Bryson for the first time since I heard his story and it's clear that he's incredibly drunk. He's swaying and his eyes are glazed and when he sees me it's clear he doesn't really recognize me but I still nevertheless decide to exchange words with the man. I say, "It's good to see you, Bryson. I still think of the story you told about your friend and his mom. It's the most powerful story I've ever heard in AA." Bryson looks away from me after I say this and begins to stumble away. As he does so he says, "I don't know. Stranger things have happened."

Zeke introduces me to customers by saying, "This man has a PhD," and I'm unsure if I loathe the behavior or find it endearing. Most customers seem impressed, marveling at me like I'm some alien species, although there are some who appear confused about what a humanities doctorate even is. "My guy is proof that drug users aren't all losers," Zeke says with paternal pride, seemingly unaware of how insulting his comment could be construed to his other customers. I luxuriate in the attention, proud to be exceptional in this domain, surrounded as I am mostly by high-school dropouts or those with one semester of college. "You're not like them," I think, as if my education has inoculated me from the ugliness of need, a thought that's staggering not just in its arrogance but in its deviation from reality. The truth is: separateness is an illusion. For better or worse separateness is an illusion and if you think you're better than someone your destiny is to be shown that you're not.

Overheard at Zeke's: "Here's the plan: we get a dog any dog it doesn't matter the breed it just can't be dumb or at least not so dumb that it can't be trained. We then pay some initial investment I don't know how much let's say like ten or fifteen thousand dollars and then anyway we get it trained at some special dog training school like one I heard about in Florida. And no it's not what you think it's not to detect bombs or drugs or anything like that the real money is if we get the dog trained to detect motherfucking *bedbugs*. Yes you heard me right bedbugs those nasty critters that are in like every homeless shelter we train a dog to detect bedbugs so that we can rent him out. The handlers charge an insane amount something like two-to-three hundred an hour I shit you not two-to-three hundred an hour for a dog to smell some furniture and clothes. Plus you have to remember that bedbugs are everywhere in this god-forsaken country and that there are actually so many places worried about them that there's a three-week waiting list to secure the dog's services. Isn't that nuts? Anyway think about it even at two hundred an hour that's a thousand every five hours which means you recoup your initial ten thousand dollar investment after fifty hours of the dog doing its thing. Do you see where I'm going with this? Are you picking up what I'm putting down? We could even split the profits if you'd like. Maybe not 50/50, but 80/20 or 70/30 or I don't know something that at least acknowledges the whole thing was my goddamn idea. I just need help with the initial investment, you know? And yes sure I know it might seem unfair to not split everything with the investor 100% down the middle. But if I'm going to do that I need proof the guy's operating in good faith, you know what I mean? Like you, for instance. I'd be happy to split everything 50/50 with you. All you'd have to do to show you're good for it is buy me a gram. Because the truth of the matter is this: I'm hard up for cash. So you buying me a gram shows me that you're serious about investing. I need that in a business partner. Seriousness. Integrity. Security in all financial matters. Yes sir. Buy me a gram and I guarantee you we'll make this fucking happen."

I've spent the night with my neighbor, Lincoln, and I'm about to leave to walk back to my house when Lincoln asks me if I've ever kissed a girl. Specifically he asks, "You ever frenched a girl?" a question that exoticizes the act and in so doing of course makes me apprehensive of the behavior. The question puts me in a bit of a bind as I'm in seventh grade and don't want to admit to having never kissed a girl but I also don't want to get caught in a lie. Eventually I decide to commit to the lie and nonchalantly affirm that I have, at which point Lincoln narrows his eyes and asks me who I kissed. I scramble to think of someone that sounds plausible, someone who I have more than an acquaintance-like relationship with and the only person I can think of is a girl I "dated" for three days in sixth grade, Holly. I say that Holly and I kissed while we were dating which causes Lincoln to narrow his eyes as he doesn't believe me but has no way of immediately falsifying the information. Plus he knows that Holly and I were attached (albeit briefly), this attachment providing the veneer of plausibility that I'd been hoping for, and after a moment of silence Lincoln evidently decides to not call me out. He says, "Yesterday I frenched Amanda for like an hour. You want to french one of Amanda's friends?" Initially I don't respond to Lincoln's question as the prospect of kissing someone makes me uncomfortable especially if that person is someone I don't know or someone I have no interest in kissing. "Who's Amanda's friend?" I ask, which Lincoln elects to not provide an answer to, instead standing up from the couch we're sitting on and gesturing for me to follow him outside. I reluctantly do what he says and the two of us walk over to a nearby park where under a canopy of trees we locate Amanda and a girl I don't know who looks our age. The girl has red hair and wears flannel and has piercing blue eyes and most importantly is morbidly obese. "Right on time!" Amanda says, a comment that demonstrates the degree of Lincoln's scheming, as he clearly orchestrated this meetup however haphazard it may appear. "This your friend?" the obese girl says, somehow scowling at the same time she obnoxiously chews on gum and after she says this Lincoln slowly nods his head. Lincoln is barely paying attention and is licking his lips while he stares at Amanda as if my presence here was a condition that had to be met in order for Amanda to agree to meet up with Lincoln again. "You guys ready to kiss?" Amanda says, and as the obese redhead scowls again she spits out her gum at which point she sighs dramatically and shrugs her shoulders. "Whatever," the redhead says. "Let's just do this already. I'm already super fucking bored." My response to hearing this is complex as I'm first amazed by how jaded the redhead seems, a level of jadedness that would seem more befitting of a seasoned vet at kissing. Which for all I know the girl might actually be. Given her extreme corpulence and age I admit that this is exceedingly unlikely but even at my age I know the world's a very peculiar place. The second element of my response involves irritation with the selfishness of Lincoln as it's now clear he's used me like a bargaining chip or some kind of sacrificial lamb. I attempt to make eye contact with Lincoln but he studiously avoids even glancing at me, ravenously eyeing Amanda as he is, as if he were poised to utterly consume her. The final element of my response consists of a slew of negative emotions—namely fear, disgust, contempt, embarrassment, anger, and self-loathing—all of which are prompted by the figure of Amanda's nameless friend. I don't want to kiss the girl and am hesitating to do so when Lincoln irritatedly asks me to hurry up. "She's willing to kiss you, Keen!" he says. "It's not like you've ever kissed a girl before!" I glare at Lincoln when he says this, astonished by the level of both his impudence and betrayal but for his part he declines to look at me whatsoever. He's licking his lips and staring at Amanda and in his mind he's alone with her right now naked in a room and it's clear to me that any level of reprimand will accomplish absolutely nothing. My hesitation continues which prompts the obese redhead to roll her eyes at which point Lincoln snaps at me, "Kiss her, Keen, or else!" It's now my turn to scowl at Lincoln who irritatingly has finally deigned to make eye contact with me though in this contact there's no acknowledgment of his betrayal. He's all but snarling at present and seems seconds away from tackling me to the ground all of which is to say his level of aggression is extremely disconcerting. With minor amounts of trepidation and major amounts of self-loathing I take four steps forward until I'm right in front of the first girl I'm ever going to kiss. I pause to reflect, to consider what one does the first time one kisses a girl but before I come to any conclusion the obese girl has enveloped me in her flesh. Her arms are folded around me and her tongue is slithering in my mouth and in fact while my eyes are closed I imagine I'm french-kissing a humanoid-like viper. The girl's tongue's repulsive rhythmic movements end after maybe five or six seconds at which point she releases me and pulls a piece of gum from her pocket. My mouth evidently is agape as Lincoln says, "Pull your jaw off the ground, Keen!" at which point he, Amanda, and the obese girl begin to cackle. This cackling only lasts a few seconds before Lincoln pounces on Amanda, the two of whom commence kissing with what looks like a great deal of both passion and skill. Eighteen months later Amanda will have given birth to a child, the father of whom I'm uncertain of, though Lincoln insists it's not his. "That bitch was slutty, dude. Total whore," Lincoln will say at the time. His eyes will be glazed as he does so and he'll be licking his lips.

"You know I have a crush on you, right?" Rachel says this outside of a bar after I've had eight IPAs and she's had much less, probably three or four. We're both students at Columbia, she in engineering and I in social work and there's been a longstanding flirtation between the two of us. This flirtation however is markedly stronger on the part of Rachel as I'm still reeling from my breakup with Zoe a year before. As a result I've been emotionally unavailable throughout this whole year in my Master's program and in fact haven't had any romantic contact with anyone. On one occasion admittedly when I was exceedingly lonely I contacted a sex worker and arranged to meet up. I got cold feet however and this year have resorted to reading long novels—*2666*, etc.—declining almost all social engagements that have presented themselves to me. Tonight however marks the end of this semester's academic calendar and I'm at a bar because Rachel asked me if I wanted to celebrate. I say, "I figured you did. I have a crush on you, too." Rachel gets a twinkle in her eye and smiles and motions for me to follow her outside and after I do so she pushes me against a brick wall in order to make out. We do this for maybe thirty seconds at the conclusion of which she says we should go to my apartment which we end up doing after I close the tab for both of us. Soon after we arrive I offer to go down on Rachel but she waves me off and says she'd prefer to have intercourse. In fact she puts the matter crudely—"I've been waiting months for us to fuck"—and we proceed to engage in said action, at first in cowgirl and then switching over to doggy-style. Thirty seconds into doggy-style I experience an upwelling of nausea, to such a degree in fact that I momentarily stop thrusting. In an especially humiliating moment I then vomit on Rachel's legs and her back, after which I fall backwards onto my ass. "Oh my God," Rachel says after which she looks at me intently, seemingly gauging how she should react based on my own reaction to what's occurred. However she likely gleans very little as my level of drunkenness has precluded the possibility of extensive communication and soon thereafter I see a resoluteness enter Rachel's eyes. "Do you have any towels?" Rachel asks, a question which prompts me to vaguely gesture at my dresser and after Rachel opens the second drawer and procures a towel she wipes the chunks of vomitus off her body. She then tosses me the second towel in my dresser and says, "Clean yourself up when you can," after which she quickly clothes herself and prepares to leave my dorm room. She hesitates however and turns to me after she places her hand on the handle of the door and then says, "Don't feel bad about this. It's not that big of a deal." The next day I'm hungover but still check the cost of flights to the West Coast and after seeing the bargains available I impulsively decide to move to Seattle. Five nights later which is my final night before flying to Seattle I meet with Rachel at her dorm room to watch the 1967 cult TV show, *The Prisoner*. We watch two episodes lying side-by-side on her bed and after the second episode is finished she says she's tired and wants to go to bed. I nod and put on my shoes and am preparing to open her door when she says, "Just for future reference: if you want to fuck a girl you have to make some kind of move." I must exhibit a look of confusion because Rachel follows up this comment with, "What I'm saying is: Michael, someday you're going to have to grow some balls."

I'm lying in bed with Peyton and preparing to go to sleep when Peyton says she has something to tell me. I reflexively say, "Sure. What's up?" and it's only after I say this that I sense Peyton's poised to make a serious disclosure. She then proceeds to explain that she'd recently written an email to Daniel, a mutual friend, and that in that email she'd confessed to having feelings for the man. This revelation produces a complex emotional reaction, the most notable feature of which is the feeling of betrayal. That is to say I feel betrayed because Peyton didn't consult with me before sending the email, a betrayal she acknowledges and apologizes for immediately. "Had you been planning on doing this?" I ask. "And when did you realize you have feelings for Daniel?" I'm especially interested in the latter because Peyton and Daniel have been close for three years, so close in fact that I've twice asked Peyton whether there is any sexual tension in their friendship. Peyton was emphatic on each occasion, insisting that the relationship was platonic and that furthermore she wasn't attracted to the man at all. "I didn't plan it," Peyton says. "And I only realized it as I was writing the email." I take Peyton at her word, certain that she wouldn't lie to me on a matter this consequential, although much later I'll revise or at least feel less certain of this assessment. In fact two years after this disclosure when Peyton and I finally throw in the towel I'll feel less certain about all manner of Peyton-related issues. Tonight however my allegiance still lies very much with Peyton and consequently I'm unwilling to consider the possibility that for whatever reason Peyton is being dishonest. One major reason for this is that in addition to feeling betrayed I'm presently overcome with the feeling of shame. Peyton's interested in fucking another man which means I'm not doing a good job of fucking her which in turn means that I'm inadequate and pathetic and defective. Besides feeling betrayed and ashamed I also feel an upwelling of anger, this latter emotion being one I've never felt comfortable expressing. My MO when experiencing anger—to direct the anger inward and then experience symptoms of depression—becomes operative, and in the days after the disclosure I feel anxious and sad to the point of being despondent. I'm so despondent in fact that I can barely communicate effectively with Peyton, communication that's of vital importance because we have to determine whether we're going to break up. The conversations are exhausting and exhaustive and in the end I say that as an adult she can obviously fuck anybody she wants but that there's no way I can be in a relationship with her if she has sex with Daniel. We weep and hold each other and prepare to end the relationship but ultimately Peyton chooses to refrain from sleeping with Daniel (even after he sends Peyton an email wherein he reciprocates her feelings). Within three months of this episode Daniel will have been outed as a predatory rapist, the information astonishing a huge number of people including me and Peyton. Daniel's brilliant and charismatic and is an important presence in the Syracuse BLM community which makes it all the more shocking when a post is created by BLM Syracuse that details the allegations. Daniel becomes a pariah immediately and loses his job as a lawyer and also loses a book deal he only recently obtained. "What does it mean," Peyton asks, "that I could be best friends with a rapist? Does it mean I'm drawn to evil people or just that Daniel is a sociopath?" In the aftermath of the revelations I ask myself a similar question as I've bonded with the man on numerous occasions and find it difficult to believe that that bonding wasn't real. My general impression of the man was always that he was kind-hearted and righteous and that although like me he was afflicted with bipolar—which made him unusually excitable when he got drunk—all in all he was fighting the good fight. It was difficult to square that image of a kindly man with Daniel being a sexual predator, not just for me but for everyone within the man's orbit. I think the reason it was difficult was that vis-à-vis Daniel one of two realities obtained, each of which reality was decidedly unsettling: Daniel was either a sociopathic monster who manipulated people who thought they weren't capable of being manipulated or alternatively he wasn't a monster but just existentially complex. That is to say the central question as I see it is whether Daniel's thoughtfulness and tenderness were all a put-on, or if in fact being thoughtful isn't incompatible with sexual predation. In any case after the allegations emerged Peyton stopped speaking to Daniel, a development for which the petty and insecure part of me was exceedingly grateful. Daniel had endangered my relationship and I wanted him to be rendered irrelevant which the allegations accomplished by severing contact between the two. But to return to the pivotal question: can a person do bad things and still be genuinely thoughtful and tender or does doing bad things means that the person's heart is ultimately evil? I don't know. My guess is the former. But the degree to which our actions implicate and condemn us is unclear. Perhaps the more important question is: do the condemned always know they're condemned? And even more importantly: is there anything they can do about it if they are?

I've gotten in the habit of brunching with Tony and his family once per month and have just now arrived at his house in order to do so. However on this particular occasion another guest is in the house, a mutual high school friend, Stu, whom I haven't seen in over a decade. Stu and I make small talk and slowly catch each other up and both of us seem to have a pleasant time doing so. Still at one point during the breakfast Stu mentions that he once worked for Lockheed Martin, a disclosure that I find to be unnerving. I instantly think of my friend, Noah, a man I love like a brother, albeit a brother who's prone to making moral judgments and to feeling righteous indignation. In fact the day after the brunch I inform Noah of what occurred, namely that a high school friend disclosed that he once worked for Lockheed Martin. Noah says, "Wow. That's insane. Did you ask any follow-up questions?" and I inform Noah that I elected not to do so. He says, "That warrants interrogation. I'd want to know what his job was and why he did it. As in, I'd want to know if he was knowingly doing something immoral." I try to talk Noah down from the ledge and explain that I was breaking bread with the man but for his part Noah won't really relent. He says, "Working for a defense contractor is fucked up. Stu should probably know that," after which I ask him at what point a person's moral contamination ends. I say, "What about people that work for Boeing? One part of Boeing manufactures weapons. Another part of Boeing, though, mainly concerns itself with airplanes. Are you saying a person is morally compromised if they're an aeronautical engineer for the airplane section? Or that you're immoral for working for Starbucks even though they're anti-union? Or what about Amazon? They exploit the workers in the warehouse. Are you immoral for working for Amazon because of the shit they put their workers through?" Noah refuses to acknowledge any nuance and insists that Lockheed Martin is shitty and that anyone who works for them is complicit in evil. I'm frustrated by his response—the man is otherwise brilliant—and consequently I try to make the issue more personal. I say, "I sometimes work with unsavory people. Murderers, rapists, drug dealers, and so on. These people have done bad things, and maybe don't deserve to be forgiven. And yet I have to forgive them. I have to believe there's something worth salvaging in these people. If I didn't, I couldn't function as a social worker." Noah says, "You need that mentality, sure. It's important for you as you do your job. I get that, and I respect the function it plays." I'm still frustrated with Noah as I regard his comment as insufficiently validating and so I continue by saying, "It's not just about my job. People aren't monolithically good or bad. Good people do bad things and vice versa." Noah seems to consider the merit of what I've said and in the end he shrugs his shoulders, at which point he says, "You're as good as your behavior. If you're good, you shouldn't do things that are bad." I disagree with Noah and feel that there's only one final tack I can take, and that's to make the issue as personal as I can. I say, "I've done bad things. I'm not perfect. I'm not as bad as the worst thing I've done," to which he says to me, "But you are, Michael. An evil man is a man who does evil things."

I'm with another intern in New York's Financial District and I'm struggling mightily just to make forgettable small talk. She's quiet and pensive and seems just generally out of sorts but because I don't yet know her I don't feel comfortable inquiring into her mental health. "How much longer do you think it will take?" I ask, gesturing at the newly-under-construction Freedom Tower and the woman seems sufficiently distracted that it's like I'm talking to myself. She shrugs her shoulders and doesn't make eye contact with me and only as an afterthought does she say, "No clue. Probably a few more years." The woman's lack of interest irritates me and consequently I'm tempted to walk in silence until we get to the hospice's main office but instead I make one last-ditch effort at small talk. I say, "They say everyone in New York knows someone affected by 9/11. Do you think that's true? And were you at all affected?" The woman clears her throat and then stares ahead, seemingly still preoccupied with whatever personal drama she's reckoning with, when she suddenly turns her head and gazes at my eyeballs. She says, "I don't know. I couldn't tell you. As for me, my father died in the Twin Towers. He was running down a stairwell, I think, when the tower imploded." I assume my mouth is agape and that I look perched somewhere between astonishment and horror because the woman continues before I can get in a word of apology. She says, "It could have been worse. He could have been burned alive. That happened to some people. Just sit and imagine that."

"Whose apartment even is this?" the girl I'm talking to asks and we both laugh because neither of us know. I'm a freshman at Berkeley and it's the night of my last fall semester final and so my intention is to celebrate by getting exceedingly drunk. The woman's a local and tells me she works at the theater on Shattuck and from the way she says it I can tell she's insecure about not being a student at the University. We talk for ten more minutes, at which point I say, "Well I guess we should each go make the rounds. Start hobnobbing or whatever. The whole thing is kind of empty, though, don't you think?" The girl shifts her head like a dog and asks me to clarify what I mean at which point I continue my line of thought. I say, "Take the two of us. We're connecting. Vibing. Flirting.

Whatever. At most parties, it's just a series of fleeting connections. You're vaguely connecting, but it goes nowhere. You end the night alone. That's the key thing. You try to connect, but you end the night alone." The girl seductively smiles and leans back and crosses her arms at which point she gives me the once over. She says, "What if you were absolutely sure you didn't have to end the night alone? Like you could do your hobnobbing but know that someone was waiting for you?" I look in the girl's eyes and she looks somehow both playful and ravenous and predictably I feel the stirrings of an erection. I say, "That'd be great. It'd be awesome. And it would make socializing way, way easier. I wouldn't feel so desperate and empty hopping from one conversation to the next." The girl's smile widens and she then kisses me on the cheek at which point she whispers to me, "Meet me in the corner bedroom at 1:30." The girl then saunters off to the kitchen and promptly joins a conversation with a man and woman holding hands at which point for my part I walk through the kitchen toward the balcony to smoke. The next three hours evaporate with the girl and I doing a kind of dance, periodically passing each other at the party and acknowledging each other only with a nod. At 1:28 the alarm on my phone goes off whereupon I excuse myself from a conversation with a math-major junior and drunkenly stagger over to the bedroom. Sure enough the girl is there and she's seductively recumbent on the bed where she gestures at me with her finger like I'm on a fishing line that she's retrieving. After I crawl onto the bed she places a condom in my hand and we proceed to make out and grope each other for thirty seconds. We then have sloppy sex—no foreplay, just immediate intercourse—during which I'm the only one of us to orgasm and after which I sit on the bed swaying from side to side. She stands up and clothes herself and then rummages through my pants and after having located it she inputs her number into my phone. She says, "I had fun. We should do this again. Preferably when you're not so drunk," words to which I nod but don't otherwise react. The truth is that I feel nauseated and am worried I'm going to puke and so consequently I move as little as possible. Eventually she blows me a kiss and leaves the room which means I'm completely and utterly alone and as it's 2 AM the party's over and I need to go back to my dorm. I struggle to contain my nausea as I gingerly put on my clothes and as I exit the bedroom I see a freshman computer science major, Brodie. He says, "Holy shit, Keen. Did you just fuck Mallory in that bedroom?" I nod but in light of my nausea don't respond in any other way. He then says, "Way to go, man. A black chick. Score one for the home team." After which I look at him blankly and say, "Yeah. The home team. Right."

I want to be an NBA player and am convinced that I will be as long as I work hard and remain singularly focused. I idolize Michael Jordan and watch as many Bulls games as I can and after the games are finished I go outside and practice shooting. I even go to a basketball camp, NBC, that has an evangelical tinge to it which is to say that at one point in the camp when every camper is in the gymnasium we're asked to accept Jesus into our hearts. I pay no mind to this idiocy and watch as the campers around me raise their hands and close their eyes, after witnessing which I remind myself that my goal is to play in the NBA. Today I had the second day of basketball tryouts at Ferrucci junior high and at day's end I learned I was cut from the team. I come home and I cry and my dad asks me why I'm upset and I tell him that I don't think I'm going to play in the NBA. He laughs and sips on his bourbon and says, "You don't want to play in the NBA," at which point, puzzled, I say, "I do. I want to be the next Michael Jordan." My father then takes another drink and vigorously shakes his head, at which point he says, "You don't stand a chance, Michael. You're not black. And you actually have a brain."

Among Zeke's many customers are Mia and Sonia, two trans women who earn money from sex work. I've met each before but neither seem to remember me nor do they exhibit much interest in me before learning I have a PhD. Mia says, "Oh, really? A PhD?" at which point she begins to speak Arabic, as if having a doctorate makes me fluent in every language on Earth. I say, "I don't know any foreign languages," which produces a sustained eye-roll on Mia's part and any interest she had in me has been immediately lost. Mia then says, "Whenever I take Xanax I take three bars at a time," and it's unclear to me what she's looking for in response. Several minutes later loosened up by two lines I ask Mia and Sonia about their involvement with sex work. "You'd be surprised," Sonia says. "It's all straight men in relationships. Unhappy straight men who have shit they need to work out." "It sure is!" Mia titters, at which point she flutters her hand across my thigh. There's so much to learn from the world that surrounds me.

"Do I strike you as transphobic?" Rebecca asks me, a question I consider absurd, especially given how much of an activist and ally the woman aspires to be. "No," I say. "Why do you ask?" She then explains to me that her current sexual partner is attracted to trans women and that furthermore this partner, Kai, has on several occasions been sodomized by such. "Okay?" I say. "So what?" Rebecca scoffs and says, "I think that's disgusting. It's not fair of me, but knowing that makes my vagina not want to work." I say, "Why do you think that is? As in, what is it about him liking trans women that's upsetting?" Rebecca says she doesn't know and then she starts to tear up, after which point she collects herself and slowly continues. "It's just gross. I don't like it. I don't want my dominant partner to be fucked in the ass." I shrug my shoulders and swig from my Rockstar after which I do my best to comfort Rebecca. I say, "You get turned on by dominant men. That's okay. Nothing wrong with that. You're not a bad liberal if sexual passivity in your partners is a turn-off." Rebecca looks at me anxiously, clearly dissatisfied by my answer and proceeds to ask me if I have any turn-ons that my past partners have been repulsed by. "No," I say. "Not really." Rebecca then says, "Okay, well do you have any sexual interests that you think a partner *would* be repulsed by?" I mull over the possibility of telling Rebecca about my interest in older women, then consider doing the same about my interest in race play and my obsession with cuckold pornography. However as these sexual interests come to mind it occurs to me that I'd never share them with a partner, mainly because I'd worry about being judged as morally deviant or disgusting. I also don't want to disclose these interests to Rebecca so I decide to feign sexual blandness which admittedly makes me guilty of lying albeit by omission. I say, "I'm pretty vanilla, Rebecca. In fact, sexually, I'm the most boring person I know. But to invert your question: I've been in your position before." Rebecca gestures at me to continue which I do by mentioning Victoria, a woman I briefly dated who was involved in the BDSM scene and enjoyed engaging in knife play. I say, "It turned me off knowing that she wanted a knife held to her throat. It wouldn't have worked long-term for that reason alone." Rebecca says, "But I need to accept this. Straight guys are going to be experimenting with trans women more and more. I don't want to think the sex acts my partner are into are repulsive." I open my mouth to speak but Rebecca instead interjects, saying, "I know, I know, I know. You were going to say that scat play is repulsive. That's what you were going to say, right?" I then say, "In a way. More or less. I was going to say that shit and piss are repulsive. But I was also thinking about what's even more repulsive than that." Rebecca looks confused and taps her finger to her lip at which point she asks, "What's more repulsive than shit and piss?" I smile and say, "Death, obviously, Rebecca. There's no topping that. There's nothing more grotesque and repulsive than death."

I've had four doubles of bourbon when I receive a phone call from Bill, a phone call I take at a Portland bar, the Standard, while my friend Emelie orders a drink. I intend to greet Bill and then sign off as I don't want to be rude to Emelie but the moment I hear his voice it's clear he's drunk and has hatched some kind of plan. He speaks loudly and slurs and seems irritated by having to explain the reason for his call as if it's a character defect of mine that I'm not telepathic. "Venmo me six hundred dollars and I'll get two 8-balls right now. And if you want this shit you're going to have to do it soon." Bill ends the phone call after he says this and my mind is instantly on high-alert and before I can Venmo him he texts me a follow-up message. "After you Venmo me the money come up to Seattle as soon as you can. Tonight, if that's in any way possible." Within seconds I've devised a plan which consists of telling Emelie I feel deeply nauseated and that consequently I'm going to have to leave. Will she believe me? I don't know. Emelie does after all have an extensive drug history and the abruptness of my departure is undoubtedly going to raise some red flags. But I don't care I'm soon gone I'm en route to my apartment whereupon once I arrive I take my dog for a walk and then brush my teeth to conceal the reek of booze. I then call a Lyft and am driven to the Enterprise rental car location where disconcertingly despite my drunken state I wave my credit card and am able to secure a vehicle. Soon I'm speeding on I-5 and chain-smoking American Spirits and listening to Pavement's "Gold Soundz" even though what I'm really doing is anticipating what that first line of coke will feel like. Bill calls me periodically and we make fun of each other's mothers but it's all theater all we care about is doing blow. Finally I arrive after having basically smoked a pack between Portland and Seattle and after meeting Bill on the street we take the elevator in his building up to his apartment. The apartment's above his means in fact I have no idea how he affords it given that it's the pandemic and he's been unemployed for many, many months. The truth is: Bill's relationship to money is bizarre and I'll never understand it even though in his own words I'm his best friend and I know everything about him. I actually don't know everything about him and that's because we never discuss how he stays financially afloat whether it's through handouts from his mother or his friends or what exactly. He's secretive in the most basic ways and I can sense that that's toxic at least it is for me because secrets make me feel unbearably lonely. But so we arrive in his apartment and I survey the amount of coke available and I'm happy to see that Bill hasn't dipped all that much into the two bags. Of course he's obviously still flying his self-control isn't absolute but if anything the cocaine he's done between the phone call and now has evened out his state. We then proceed to bond in our hetero way our way that integrates put-downs, jokes, reminiscences, movie references, and warmth, and the blow facilitates all of this and makes it a magical experience. Or at least it's magical for the first few lines by which I mean three or maybe even two or what am I talking about the only truly magical moment is when the light bulb first turns on after that first hallowed line. Over the course of the next six hours Bill and I polish off one of the 8-balls after which point I make it clear that I have to return to Portland. My dog needs to eat and be taken for another walk which means that despite having not slept and despite being coked out of my skull I have to start the three-hour drive back. I convince Bill to accompany me and by 8:30 AM we're on our way and throughout the drive we either bump cocaine or gum it off our fingers. We sing along to Outkast and Dr. Dre and other rap music from our youth and throughout the drive I only almost get into two accidents. By the time we arrive in

Portland I'm eager to do an actual line but when we exit the car Bill tells me we've already consumed the entirety of the other 8-ball. I call bullshit on the man not knowing how that's possible and a wedge is created between us because I'm convinced Bill hid away a gram before we left. We proceed to bicker about God knows what, a direct consequence of being out of coke, as the euphoria is wearing off and I'm certain that being out means I've been lied to. I don't directly accuse him of malfeasance but he knows something's wrong and when he asks me why I'm agitated I blame the lack of coke. Eventually we sleep after which we wake and head to a bar straightaway, a bar I select based on research I've conducted on Yelp on Portland bars that are notorious for coke. We're unsuccessful in our mission though I eye everyone at the bar we end up going to and on two occasions almost broach the subject to patrons who are blotto. Bill then suggests we get Kratom which is a drug I've never done and one I assume will not affect me whatsoever. Nevertheless I agree and soon we're back at my apartment and within ten minutes I've consumed fifty percent of a $30 bag. I proceed to get so stoned that I first vomit and then dry heave after which point I enter a twilight state for twelve hours between wakefulness and sleep. It's not fun I hate myself I feel debased by my addict-like impulses and all I want right now is for Bill to go back to Seattle. I feel haggard and hollowed out and at the moment of Bill's departure I have nothing to spare, no cleverness, no parting repartee, nothing at all. We both want to be alone or at least not in the company of each other as there's a sloppiness to a drug binge that makes you feel like you've shared too much and now need to retreat. That is to say you want to retreat from the world, from your friends, from your mind, you want to sleep it off and feel like you were never even here. Because you weren't and you aren't this whole thing called your life is an illusion it's a game you're playing because you have nothing else to do.

In the last two months I've been sexually involved with three women, Leslie, Jennifer, and Tamara. Leslie's the youngest of the three and is a graduate student in Syracuse's Visual and Performing Arts Program although despite having slept with her twice I can't tell you anything about her art. We met at a local dive, Taps, and slept together the night that we met and as is true of many drunken encounters I remember very little about what occurred. What I can say however—and I regard this as both sad and unnerving— is that on the second occasion we sleep together Leslie begins crying in the middle of the sexual act. When we stop and debrief she apologizes for her "weirdness," only saying that she was traumatized by a recent sexual partner. Years later I'll learn from a friend living in Portland, Gina, that this partner was Julian, a disgraced member of my MFA cohort who was kicked out of the program for sexual misconduct. My relationship with Leslie in any case never gained any real traction in part because Leslie wanted to remain single but also because she felt embarrassment about crying. The second woman, Jennifer, is a barista I dated my first year in Syracuse, one with whom early on I knew there was no long-term potential. We spent six anodyne months together at the conclusion of which I ended the relationship, an action I renege on when while intoxicated I text her to come over to have sex. She agrees to come over and during the sexual act I say, "I love you," words I never said to her even in the midst of our relationship. Jennifer passionately reciprocates which makes the post-coital period extremely heavy and as I look at her I know I have to acknowledge what's just occurred. In a shameful (but necessary) move I confess to Jennifer to having lied or at least to having been "carried away" by my passion when I said what I did. "You said you love me," Jennifer asks, "but you don't actually love me?" Jennifer leaves in a huff when I affirm that yes in fact this is the case and in the weeks that follow she becomes incredibly angry. The final woman I sleep with, Tamara, is newly out of a relationship and is going through an extended mental health episode. The campus psychiatrist has been prescribing her various antidepressants and mood stabilizers—lithium, Effexor, Lamictal, etc.— none of which are improving Tamara's emotional state whatsoever. An English PhD student, Tamara initially reaches out to me as a friend as she knows I'm both a social worker and someone who has struggled with his own mental health. However at the beginning of the summer, not long after I sleep with first Leslie and then Jennifer, Tamara confesses to having romantic feelings for me. I express apprehension about getting involved as Tamara's mental health is decidedly poor but she insists that her feelings for me are unrelated to her illness. Tamara says, "I like you despite my mental problems, not because of them," and I take her at her word and before long I'm functioning as both Tamara's lover and emotional caregiver. We create a codependent cocoon and soon I've isolated myself from all my friends but I don't care because Tamara and I are in love with a capital L. We watch *True Detective* and smoke pot and drink Maker's Mark and have sex and talk about art, God, mental illness, and etc. Soon we're talking about marriage and Tamara says she would say yes if I proposed so today we went to a jeweler and Tamara picked out a ring. I put down a thousand non-refundable dollars and I don't care it doesn't matter all that matters is that Tamara and I maintain our cocoon. I want to celebrate in some capacity I want to acknowledge the momentousness of the day especially because it's Halloween, a day that already occasions a celebration. Fortunately there's an MFA party that's been planned that's due to occur at Jim and Kurt's house, a party I'm intent on bringing Tamara to so that we can gloat about our future. Tamara however is reluctant as she's a homebody and doesn't care for certain members of my program and try as I might I'm unable to convince her to attend. However she does encourage me to attend going so far as to insist that I do so and though I want to spend time with her I do eventually concede the point. I make the rounds after I arrive, telling no one about the engagement ring I purchased, and eventually I find myself on the second floor in Jim's room with Jim and a woman in my program, Peyton. The three of us smoke pot and Jim regales us with an incoherent story, one involving his time in first Mississippi and then the Marines and etc. Throughout the story Peyton laughs and for my part I also laugh at Jim's insane rendering of events and the moment is pleasant enough (if forgettable) until I look up and make eye contact with Peyton. The moment I do so something inside me shatters which is to say that I feel drawn to Peyton in a way I've never felt drawn to anyone except Zoe. A sunderance is thus created, one in which my relationship with Tamara is doomed as any feelings I have for her have been displaced by the feelings I have for Peyton. My immediate response to this is panic and in my panicked state I call Tamara and tell her to pick me up from the party. After she does so we drive away and I explain what happened with Peyton or at least attempt to do so in my presently stoned and bumbling manner of speech. While Tamara's obviously deflated she's also the only one of the two of us who seems able to accept the seismic emotional shift that's occurred. In the weeks that follow I tell myself all manner of lies and convince myself that my relationship with Tamara will survive. It will only be two months later after I realize that my feelings for Peyton have increased that I accept that my relationship with Tamara is dead. Years later when I get sober I'll recall the denial I was in for this two-month period and I'll recall it if not fondly then at least with grace and acceptance in my heart. Because the truth is: I was knee-deep in denial yes but I've spent my whole life in denial and the only recipe I've found for happiness is acceptance of the present moment including whatever state of denial I'm in. Or phrased another way: there's no understanding the human heart. It will defy you and upend you. It will serve as a mirror and say, "You're nothing. You're what I tell you to be."

It's 2002 and I'm walking across the border to Tijuana and within seconds it feels like I've entered another dimension. Words and phrases pop through my skull— "Hades," "netherworld," "den of iniquity," etc.—all of which I check myself for because I'm otherizing the city. I tell myself, "Tijuana's just like any other city," as I walk down a boulevard where seemingly everyone is drunk and mariachi music fills the air everywhere I go. I'm with Aaron who's ten years older and who drove from the Zen center we're staying at to the Mexican border and after he orders drinks for us he tells me he has two objectives. He says, "I want to get you some pussy, and I want to get myself cocaine," after which point he takes a shot of bourbon and gestures at a glass and asks me to do the same. I comply with the request and soon we've migrated to a second bar wherein we have several shots before leaving to go to the next location. "Alright," Aaron says, "It's time to go to a strip club. The bartender told me one we could go to where I can get some coke." We then teeter over to some dingy strip club where Aaron talks to the bartender and then disappears at which point I'm left alone at the bar. Soon thereafter I'm approached by a stripper with dreadlocks, dreadlocks which make me briefly consider the issue of cultural appropriation. "Quiero blowjob," I yell at the woman, and she gestures with her hand for me to reduce my volume, which I do by repeating my words in a whisper. Soon I've paid the requisite number of pesos and I'm alone in what looks like a dressing room at one end of the bar and I drunkenly wait for the dreadlocked stripper to appear. Soon the curtain is pulled open and the stripper stands above me looking impassive if not somewhat bored and after closing the curtain she guides my pants off and puts a condom on my dick. "I've never gotten a blowjob with a condom," I say although the truth is that I've never received oral sex in any capacity and that consequently the peculiarity of the situation doesn't fully compute at the present moment. "No hablo inglés," the stripper says and I find the language barrier to be of some measure of comfort, in large part because it will ensure that the tryst will be as transactional as possible. The dreadlocked stripper then fellates me and given how drunk I am it's shocking I'm able to cum but I do and then the stripper disappears. I shimmy back into my clothing and exit the dressing room and when I find Aaron smiling from ear to ear I ask him if he was able to secure cocaine. "I sure did," Aaron says and fifteen minutes later we've left the bar and as we're walking back toward the American border I ask him what cocaine feels like. Aaron says, "It makes you feel how you want to feel," an opaque statement if I've ever heard one but one that intrigues me sufficiently that I know I'll never forget it. "So you're saying it feels good?" I ask which prompts Aaron to nod his head. "Fuckin A it feels good. You'll find out some day. I sense cocaine is in your future."

I cut out two lines, one twice the size of the other, and after taking the larger line pass the dollar bill to Bill. We're in my apartment and it's the night of my relapse and Bill is expressing gratitude for me not succumbing to AA brainwash. "What do you mean?" I ask and he shrugs his shoulders as he accepts the bill at which point he snorts up his line and says AA is a cult. He says, "The God talk, among other things. Don't you have a problem with that? Believing in a higher power is bullshit, and you know it." As I mull over the man's comment I consider what tack I should take before it eventually dawns on me that there's no reconciling our positions. Bill can't see beyond himself and he regards transcendence as foolish or at least it seems to me that's how he feels in his bones. There is no movement beyond the self and we're all marooned in our skulls and the belief in interconnectedness is a pathology, little more than wish-fulfillment and delusion. Or so Bill would say as I know the man well and the truth is I just can't convince the man otherwise. How could I? By saying there's meaning, there's hope, that it's possible to escape the island of the self, that communion is good and desirable, that it's the raison d'être of us all? Loneliness might be the elemental scourge, the most basic of psychic afflictions, but it also might not be, I might not understand what it means to be a human being. Maybe Bill is right maybe this whole enterprise is botched and random it's hard to reject that conclusion but it just feels so sad and unacceptable to me. Altruism and transcendence those are all that really matter I think, I don't say this to Bill I just say that I think AA is misunderstood. He again shrugs his shoulders as he doesn't feel the need to pursue the issue any further and neither do I for my part I just want to embody selflessness in how I live. But for now it's time to do another line one where my line is two-or-three times the size of Bill's as this is my coke not his and he's lucky to get any because this shit is expensive.

I've just landed in Spokane, Washington, a city I have negligible interest in exploring and in fact I am only here at all to visit my girlfriend, Peyton's, father. Peyton's prepped me extensively for the visit as her father suffers from brain cancer and even more than this as part of his affliction has had one-third of his brain removed. "He's been studied by a bunch of people," Peyton says. "He's lived longer with his form of cancer than anyone in history." When I express admiration for this Peyton looks unimpressed and shrugs her shoulders. "I guess it's cool," she says. "But he's basically a child. He doesn't know what basic words mean, like 'helicopter' or 'avocado.'" In the leadup to the Spokane visit Peyton also tells me about the various other ways her father's impaired, most notably in the way he interacts with other people. She says, "He'll ask to give a hug to the cashier at Trader Joe's. Or to the post office worker. It's fucking embarrassing." I imagine what this would be like, to be able to disregard all sense of measuredness, of social decorum, and when I ask her how people respond she says, "I don't know. They're usually cool with it." I say, "Sounds pretty good to me. You get to receive hugs everywhere you go," to which Peyton says, "Yeah, but he still has brain cancer, Michael." We take a Lyft from the airport to Peyton's father's house and en route I become convinced our driver is a serial killer, as evidenced by his deviation from the app's suggested route and the fact that we seem to be in some sort of forest. I'm frantically considering exit strategies, ways to incapacitate our driver, etc., when we exit the forest and seem to be only five minutes away from her father's house. "He's going to ask to give you a hug," Peyton says. "And then he's going to say, 'I love you.' He's going to do that the moment you meet." I understand this intellectually and that I have nothing to fear from the interaction—why fear interacting with a child?—but nevertheless I'm still nervous about meeting my girlfriend's father. Soon we're on the man's doorstep and we ring the doorbell and my heart is pounding and then he's in front of us and Peyton's giving him a hug. He then hesitates when he sees me and says, "Hi, Michael. Can I give you a hug?" which he does, followed by telling me he loves me. "I love you, too," I say, and I both mean it and don't, which come to think of it makes it like every other declaration of love I've made in my life.

"Let's play a party game," Daniel says. "A bonding exercise. A way to get to know each other." There are six of us standing on a patio as Daniel says this and though the request seems anodyne enough I experience a sinking feeling. Nevertheless people seem open to the suggestion and Daniel proposes we confess the worst thing we've ever done, a proposition that horrifies me but that I steel myself up to do. The first two people to respond claim that they don't have any major skeletons in their closet, that they're guilty of infidelity but nothing worse than that. Eventually it's time for Wendy, a first-year in the MFA program, to confess and after hemming and hawing for a short period of time she divulges a story about when she was homeless as a teenager. During this low point when she was a junkie Wendy was constantly fiending for money and enduring withdrawal which led her on one occasion—her body is noticeably tense as she confesses this—to kick and beat a homeless man in an alley in order to steal his money. She says, "It was horrible, but I was a drug addict. I would have done anything to get more heroin." At this point it's my turn and I confess to seducing, and then sleeping with, a woman I met at a bar, a woman who was sufficiently drunk that I feel like I took advantage of her. Admittedly I was also drunk and after we had sex she gave me her number and encouraged me to contact her in the future but still despite this I felt like there was an imbalance in our states of intoxication. I say, "If a person's more drunk than you, you shouldn't sleep with them. A violation occurred even if she didn't regard it as a violation." I'm teary as I confess this so everyone gives me the benefit of the doubt and assures me that people have sex all the time while in differing states of intoxication. The final participant in the game is Gina, a second-year poet, and although she claims she isn't guilty of any major moral transgression she does say that she has one experience that elicits significant regret. Gina recounts that in the memory she's five years old and on the beach and she's building a sandcastle with a boy she's only just met that day and that at some point the boy tells her something she finds impossible to process. The boy that is to say relays the story of how his older brother has the boy suck on the brother's penis late at night and how after doing this for a short period he, the boy, swallows liquid that comes out of the brother's penis. In other words in this memory the boy confesses to Gina to being sexually abused but tragically the boy is so young as to not be aware of the trauma that's being enacted. The same is true for Gina, as at the time all she knows is that the story makes her uneasy, and it's only years later that she'll tell her parents about what was told to her by a random boy on the beach. The story's disquieting and we're all eager to put this "party game" behind us though it feels fitting that someone offer a capping phrase to officially end the episode. Daniel says, "Wendy and Michael, you're the winners," and I don't know precisely what he means, maybe that we're bad people or that we're interesting or more likely that the two terms are one and the same.

I'm seated in the center of an auditorium at a table with two other students in my class while the hundred-odd other students observe the three of us discuss interracial dating. We've been given minimal instructions by our professor, Dr. Li—"Just talk about anything related to interracial dating as it relates to your experience"—which perhaps inevitably leads to a discussion of our respective dating histories. The first person to speak, a southern white woman, utters some bromide about how she supports interracial dating but that she doesn't have any personal experience in doing so. I volunteer to speak next and say that I have minimal (but some) experience with interracial dating but that like any non-bigoted person I'm open to the possibility of dating outside of my race. In an attempt to complexify the conversation however I add that while I'm open to dating outside of my race there are other factors that would make a partnership unlikely. "It's unlikely," I say, "that I'd date someone who doesn't have a high school diploma. I'm not opposed to it, but education and culture provide a lot of common ground." I'm trying to cut through liberal posturing in other words, one that feigns open-heartedness and acceptance when in fact liberals are also guilty of bias, bigotry, judgment, and discrimination. The third member of the conversation, a middle-aged black man, seems refreshingly unconcerned with toeing some liberal line and he confesses to having never dated outside of his race and not being open to doing so. He makes an argument adjacent to mine—"I want someone to share my culture with me. That's only feasible if the woman is black."—but his tone is more unapologetic than mine which is to say he sees no drawbacks to his position. And maybe there aren't. I don't know. In any case I have no interest in lecturing a black man about his cultural myopia or narrow-mindedness, nor do I have much interest in shaming the man when he was courageous enough to be honest. What's remarkable however is the southern woman's response, a response that seems to be predicated on or at least emboldened by the words of the black student. She says, "I wouldn't date outside of my race, either. Not because I'm against it in any way. Someone outside of my race just wouldn't be accepted by my family." The woman strikes me as naïve and unaware and, unlike the other student, still concerned with the impression she's making but when I look for any negative reaction in the black student I find nothing. Nevertheless the truth-seeking part of me—and if I'm honest a sadistic part of me as well—wants to cut through the southern woman's performative bullshit. I say, "But that's functionally racist, right?" The woman looks confused by my comment, clearly convinced that I'm guilty of some basic misunderstanding, a misunderstanding I'll be disabused of if she clarifies her position. She says, "No, not at all. I'm not against interracial dating, even for myself. It's just like I said. I wouldn't do it because it would upset my family." I say, "But if your family isn't open-minded, and you always act in accordance with your family, then by extension you're acting in a way that isn't open-minded. Right?" I raise the question quietly, unobtrusively, and I closely examine the woman for her reaction and as I do so I observe a pathetic affective evolution. She starts out disbelieving and uncomprehending, unsure of how I could so dramatically misunderstand her position, and then moves to red-faced indignation before finally yielding to shame. "I'm sorry! I'm sorry!" the woman keens as the waterworks begin and after they do Dr. Li wisely ends the class. Outside of the auditorium I run into a classmate I'm on friendly terms with, Jen, and ask her whether she thought my behavior during the exercise was inappropriate. "Yes and no," Jen says. "You were making a good point. But you could have been nicer about it. She is a country girl, after all." I say, "Nicer about it? How? I was quiet and didn't raise my voice. How would I say what I want to say in a way that she'd consider nice?" Jen considers the question and sighs. She says, "Maybe you're right. There really was no way of winning. So to answer your question: you were in the right, but everyone still thinks you're an asshole." I say, "Do you think I'm an asshole?" Jen first shrugs her shoulders and then smirks. She then says, "How would I say what I want to say in a way that you'd consider nice?"

Six months of near-sobriety and all I've done is pace in my apartment which is all I can do during Covid and after my breakup with my fiancée. I'm poised to return to Louisiana to take an exam for my PhD program it'll feel like a homecoming albeit a homecoming to a place I associate with her. The situation's fraught and I wake up with my jaw hurting every morning presumably because I've been grinding my teeth while I sleep. The night before I fly I have a conversation with a man in my building, Nick, a portly computer programmer who appears to have autistic tendencies. He mentions "partying" the previous weekend and my cocaine-antennae begin to tingle at which point I invite him to the building's patio to share some Lagavulin. He accepts the invitation and within minutes I've asked him if he can get cocaine and he avers that he can through his lawyer friend, Doug. We both get drunk and Nick vomits and after I escort him to his room I ruminate on Covid, my life, and this sad, disintegrated world. The next day I fly to Lafayette and a hurricane arrives soon thereafter, an event that feels freighted with meaning in an obvious, numbskull kind of way. However for my part I don't care as I'm more concerned with showing off the weight I've lost, a development I think will convince people that I've fully recovered from the breakup. Of course the opposite is true if anything I'm still gutted by the loss of Peyton and nothing cosmetic is going to change that at all. But being in Lafayette is overwhelming which is exactly how I knew it would be which makes it unsurprising that I go hog wild on cocaine. The plug I find, Skywalker, is a man I meet through a friend of mine, Courtney, and I buy three 8-balls in eight days which is a testament to my precarious mental state. During the eight days of use I do cocaine with maybe eight or nine people and invariably when I do I talk about how I'm coping with the loss of Peyton. Of course I'm actually processing nothing as the cocaine inoculates me from anything resembling vulnerability which is to say I can say vulnerable things without feeling weak in any way. And I do say vulnerable things, I talk about childhood rape, Peyton, bipolar, and so on, all the while fixating on my diminishing euphoria and how long it is until my next line. In fact that's the only reason I don't collapse during my visit, it's what allows me to proceed as if everything is totally fine, which is to say the single-minded determination on my part to do the next (and next and next and next) line of cocaine. And yes while I hobnob and laugh and get brunch with an old coworker in downtown Lafayette I'm still fundamentally broken, so much so that I listen to Lana Del Rey's "Let Me Love You Like a Woman" on repeat the entire time that I'm there.

And my heart is so full or my heart is so empty I don't know it just feels like it's spider-cracked glass that's poised to shatter at any moment. In the end I do what I need to do and see the people I need to see and then I return to Portland after my coke binge ready to do even more coke. Doug and I hit it off like gangbusters and begin to regularly do blow and within two weeks he's introduced me to his friend, Guy. Guy I soon learn is a former professional football player who smokes crystal meth every day and also experiences auditory hallucinations. He takes Abilify, an antipsychotic, which incidentally is the same antipsychotic I've taken for over a decade although I take it for bipolar and am on a much smaller dosage. The second time I meet Guy he meets me at my shoebox apartment alone as Doug is delayed because he's spending time with his girlfriend. Guy and I talk about god knows what and it occurs to me that he could easily kill me after all he's got a hundred pounds on me and every inch of it is muscle. He's gentle and soft-spoken but he's also capable of aggression or so it seems based on his time in the NFL as a defensive end. What's also unnerving is that Guy's father is in prison for murder, in this case for going on a rampage at a law school that left three people dead. Guy's father from what I gather was in the midst of a psychotic episode when he went on the spree which of course is chilling because Guy's hallucinations also mark him as psychotic. I'm anxiously considering all of this when Guy ushers me back to reality which he does by asking me if I want to smoke meth. I shrug my shoulders and agree and soon I've got a meth pipe in my mouth and Guy's holding a blow torch to heat up the meth that's in the pipe. "How do you feel?" Guy asks thirty seconds later and while this is polite he doesn't seem all that interested in what I have to say. I consider the question and as I do so it occurs to me that this moment on crystal meth is the clearest and most lucid I've felt in my entire life. Guy's term for crystal meth, "clear," suddenly seems deeply apropos and I compare this experience on meth to what I feel like on cocaine. I ultimately conclude that cocaine is speedier than meth which is to say that meth imparts lucidity without the manic quality of cocaine. Of course this is also dosage-dependent as I'm comparing the effect of three hits of crystal meth to that of an all-night coke binge which isn't really fair. My thoughts continue to brilliantly effloresce or so it seems to me at the time until Doug arrives and me, Guy, and him proceed to discuss the Bible. We talk about the beatitudes and Paul and Judas and the crucifixion and for a brief period it feels like we're making headway in a way that even theologians can't. Doug tells me I need to do more of the meth but instead of smoking it I need to eat it yes according to Doug eating meth is the only way to ensure I hallucinate in the way that I should. "That doesn't appeal to me," I say though of course it does to some degree, there's something profoundly appealing about completely losing one's bearings in this fragmented, shadow-heavy world. The rest of the night is fine with us at one point walking to a nearby Plaid Pantry, this in order to obtain cigarettes and to get out in the open air. Guy confesses to erectile dysfunction which utterly floors me as he's a hulking specimen who likely has inexhaustible sexual options. I feel a twinge of sadness for the man or maybe not sadness but compassion though of course there's a component of the former in the latter. I end the night alone as I do each night even when I'm with another person and I masturbate though I don't feel especially compelled to do so. "You have to cum on meth. It'll be the best orgasm you've ever had." Doug says this before he leaves which is what prompts me to open Pornhub minutes later and as it turns out he's right my orgasm on meth is unlike any other orgasm I've ever had. "What am I doing with my life?" I say as I wipe the cum off my stomach and to this day I don't know and I wonder what it would even look like if I did.

"There you are," Jessica, a coworker, says as she sips on tequila at the bar and I apologize for being late even though I'm here at the agreed upon time. She says, "No need to apologize. I came here an hour early. You need to catch up if you want to make this a date." I then order a double of bourbon and within an hour have completed two more of the same, at which point I ask Jessica if she wants to go back to her apartment. She orders two shots to go and after we take them I pick up the bill, this even though the two of us make shit money working for Barnes & Noble. Ten minutes later we're in her apartment, each of us with a gin and soda in our hands, and I'm admiring the impeccable job she's done decorating. I say, "Your apartment looks great," to which she responds, "Of course it does. I'm a girl," and after I laugh she sets down her glass and shifts over on the couch to straddle me. We kiss for several minutes during which time I first stick my fingers inside her and then rub her clit, after which point she says, "You better fuck the shit out of me, Michael." The moment Jessica says this I know I won't be able to maintain an erection, the reason for which is that I find aggressiveness to be a turn-off. Why this is I don't know but past experience has given me enough data to confirm that going forward my dick will be dead in the water. We nevertheless go through the motions which involve first Jessica grinding on my dick and then afterward her fellating me for several minutes to no effect. Eventually she sits back next to me on the couch and side-eyes me with disgust after which I apologize for my sexual failure. She says, "I'm fucking hot. You should be hard as shit. Seriously: what exactly is wrong with you?" And after considering the question thoughtfully I say, "Where do you want me to begin?"

Loraine says, "The first thing to know is that I'm a playwright who's known all around New York City. And the second is that I have breast cancer that's metastasized everywhere." Loraine places a Dorito in her mouth after she says this and then gestures at what looks like a brochure on the kitchen's island, after which she says, "That's for my one-person play. It's about me dying. Which I am, supposedly." I compliment the brochure, this though it looks decidedly amateurish, to which Loraine says, "Thank you. I designed it myself." Loraine proceeds to unload, talking to me about her childhood and family and lovers, at no point asking me a single question about myself. She does however eventually talk about her "wonderful hospice care team," singing the praises of each member. The one exception to this is the doctor whom Loraine claims to take issue with for the sole reason that the doctor doesn't endorse Loraine's use of non-approved medications. She says, "Chemo, radiation—it's all bullshit. I take what they prescribe me, but it does nothing. My *real* medicine, Marcus, is snake venom." I open my mouth to remind Loraine of my name when she misperceives my intentions and suddenly interjects. She says, "You seem nice enough. And I'm happy to work with you, Marcus. I just have one rule: don't *fuck* with my snake venom." I then nod as does Loraine at which point the matter seems to have been settled. She then says, "Oh and one other thing. You're going to have to read my play."

Chris has a beard and a tie-dye shirt and tells me he's on testosterone replacement therapy but what's most important is that he's stingy with his humongous bag of coke. "I don't produce T on my own," Chris tells me as he shakes out coke onto his cell phone case, at least enough for a moderate-sized line for himself. He says, "Sometimes the body needs help. And that's what I'm doing. I'm giving my body the help that it needs." I idly ask questions about where he injects the testosterone, his dosage, the side effects, etc., but of course it's all just an elaborate attempt at manipulation. I need to appear void of desire, this so that Chris doesn't feel threatened by the violence of my appetite for drugs, and my hope is that if he feels safe he'll offer me a sizable line. Soon the conversation segues to astronomy and quantum physics and I nod along avidly to his impossible-to-follow babbling which among other things involves a discussion of muons, black holes, dark energy, the multiverse, quantum fluctuations, and Schrodinger's cat. "That's crazy!" I repeatedly yell, each time more desperate than the last, waiting for Chris' magnanimity to take hold. But it doesn't and it won't and I hate him for it just as I hate everyone who doesn't give me exactly what I want which in this case is line after line of cocaine. So what can I do but smile both at Chris and the world at large yes I can smile and convince myself I'm not empty and that I care. At least almost.

It's early afternoon and I'm at Zeke's and in short order I've done three burly lines and I'm barely paying attention to some doggerel Chris has read me. It's not verse and it's not prose but instead is their bastard child, an allegory, and though he reads for five or six minutes I retain absolutely nothing. "What do you think?" Chris asks me, and I can see he wants me to validate his insipid and saccharine story, which of course I will because I see no other option. After all what would I even say if I were honest? That his story is puerile and pathetic? That it's laughable? That it belongs in a very large fortune cookie? No. I may have sadistic impulses but they're not particularly strong. In fact I feel a kinship with Chris, as the man's clearly attempting to bond with me, and as I think of how I can reciprocate I suddenly recall the end of one of my dozen-odd novels. I pull up this final section on my phone, my hand trembling from the rapid intake of three lines, and I survey my audience—Zeke in his recliner, and Chris on the beanbag chair—before I start reading my piece. Predictably it's a disaster. I've profoundly misread my audience and as I continue reading I wonder which Chris and Zeke are experiencing more of: indifference or antipathy. It's impossible to tell as my eyes are riveted on my iPhone screen and it's only out of pride that I don't stop my reading halfway through. When I do eventually finish I look first at Zeke who's at my right and I'm stunned to see he's fallen asleep. Here I am amped up on coke and baring my soul to these two men and one of them can't even tolerate three minutes of my prose. I would be humiliated were I not flying but I am flying and feel invincible to psychic pain and I then turn my attention over to Chris. His head is tilted to the side canine-like and he seems unable to process what he's heard and eventually he shrugs his shoulders and says, "Hey, you mind cutting me another line?"

It's 1 AM and I'm drunk and I've just gotten home from the Syracuse dive bar, Taps, and before going to bed I admire the books on my bookshelf. I pull out the occasional book—*Blood Meridian, Journey to the End of the Night*, etc.—and read half a page of its prose, at the conclusion of which I gently close the book and place it back on my bookshelf. Eventually I pull out a book by a Brooklyn author and read the bio on the back of the book and in doing so am reminded that the author lives in New York City. "I could meet the guy," I say out loud after which point I open my computer and go to the author's website whereupon soon thereafter I obtain the man's contact information. I impulsively then send the man an email telling him I'm an admirer of his work and I ask him if he'd be willing to get together. He's curt in his response the following day which retrospectively makes sense given that my email provided no identifying information and simply asked to get drinks. I'm much more open in my response to his response and attempt to reassure the author by establishing commonality which I can do because my rich lawyer uncle, Bernie, is a running partner of the author's father. He responds to this email kindly and we make plans to meet the following weekend which we do in Brooklyn at a bar that the author recommends. Before meeting with the author I have dinner with my historian friend, Andy, and his wife, Reiko, during which dinner I consume an entire bottle of wine. That is to say I'm drunk when I meet the man, a fact I'm uncertain whether the author can glean when we shake hands, and over the course of the next few hours we have a free-flowing conversation. We rate all manner of writers—he dislikes Sebald but admires Denis Johnson—and discuss the general state of the literary landscape and throughout I drunkenly try to keep up. At one point we're on the patio of a bar where smoking isn't permitted but the author nevertheless chooses to light an American Spirit. Soon thereafter a patron at a table seated behind us asks the author to put out his cigarette. He grumblingly complies but appears to be seething with rage, rage I'm well-accustomed to but still unnerved by because of my father. The author then shares a story about an ex who while dating him had an affair with a famous writer, a writer he doesn't name but that apparently teaches at an MFA program in New York City. The author recounts—with some pride—that when he learned of the affair he went to the writer's house and beat the shit out of the man. That writer was married and incidentally was with his family when the beating was given, a fact that shocks me but that the author seems unaffected by. Presumably he was proud of emasculating the man in front of his family, an emasculation he, the author, also undoubtedly felt when he learned his then-girlfriend was cheating on him. At no point in the night does he evince even the slightest vulnerability, as if his mind is a fortress I don't yet deserve access to. As the night wears on I become exceedingly drunk and embarrassingly I feel myself slurring and starting to nod off. The author not surprisingly becomes irritated and/or bored—I'm not sure because I'm too drunk to be attentive—and we part ways unceremoniously, never to speak again. Interestingly in the years that follow, when I look back on that night, I don't primarily think of the author's anecdotes or his anger or my drunkenness. What I think of mainly is a moment when he was shit-talking MFA programs, bemoaning the mediocrity of the work that's produced. "But that's not the fault of MFAs," I say. "Most artists are mediocre. Why would the artists at an MFA program be any different than artists in the general population?" The author says, "Well I didn't need an MFA. And I've never met a single writer who has one who was worth a damn." He says this flatly, not seeming to recognize (or at least care) that his statement implicates me, and I consider drawing his attention to how insulting his comment is. But before I say a thing I think about the work I've produced thus far—all derivative—and sadly and silently acknowledge that I too am likely condemned to be forever mediocre. At which point after this thought I take a drink of my bourbon double and say, "Actually, yeah. You're probably right."

It's the night of my thirty-seventh birthday—my first birthday after my breakup with Peyton—and I'm distraught over a text exchange we had earlier in the day. After having not communicated for several months Peyton texted me asking me whether I'd turned our Lafayette friends against her because evidently after I left Louisiana Peyton had been effectively shunned. Under the best of circumstances Peyton's text could be described as self-involved but what truly staggered me was again that the text was sent on my birthday. I tell myself I should be furious but instead I just feel lonely and sad and because I'm not angry I go to great lengths to reassure Peyton. Now it's twelve hours later and I'm alone in my apartment and I'm pacing back and forth between doing rails of cocaine. I've got Jeff Tweedy's "Love Is the King" on repeat and I keep on listening to the end of the first verse—"Life isn't fair/Love is the king"—and I'm so high that it feels like I'm on the verge of an overdose. I send Peyton a long series of texts, none of which are hostile or angry, but all of which predictably evince a deep loneliness and sadness. I also during the coke binge pore over a series of sticky notes, love-inflected notes that Peyton wrote to me at the height of our relationship. I'm existentially adrift and genuinely don't care whether I live or die which is terrifying given that I have an 8-ball to myself. At 5 AM my time when I'm preparing to go to bed I receive a lengthy response from Peyton. She's kindly enough but ends her message with incoherent spiritual gibberish, gibberish that sounds completely out of character for her. "She's not the person she was," I say to myself, neglecting to realize that I'm not the person I was either, that time makes us into infants or goldfish or some other stupid creature that lacks the capacity to remember, even if you want to which deep down I'm guessing most people don't.

Richard is tall and gregarious but gets easily winded because he's suffering from congestive heart failure. I've been his hospice social worker for six months and he says he doesn't think he has "more than a week to live," which seems dramatic but for all I know he's right. His wife is seated next to him on a couch and is talking about the logistics related to Richard's funeral which admittedly is a morbid discussion to have in front of Richard. She's talking about who she needs to call, who will be invited, etc., and throughout her monologue I closely observe Richard's expression. It's utterly opaque and consequently I project all manner of emotions onto Richard, including anger, hatred, sadness, and self-pity. Eventually Richard's wife turns to him and asks him if he has any thoughts on the matter which is a comic gesture given that she's probably just held forth for close to ten minutes. Richard says, "Whatever you think is best," which seems to frustrate Richard's wife and she then asks him if it's upsetting hearing about the details of his funeral. Richard says, "Not really, no. It's kind of comforting, actually. It makes me feel like I'll be here a bit longer, even when I'm already gone." Richard's wife then places her hand in his and says, "Honey, you'll never be completely gone," to which Richard says, "Don't be stupid. The whole point of this is that one day I completely disappear."

I'm at Zeke's talking to Mia when a man, Ricky, walks in the door, a man who causes Mia to turn to me, shake her head, and roll her eyes. She then leans in and lowers her voice, speaking sotto voce about how much she hates this man, Ricky, about how he hates trans people and has always been rude to her. Ricky for his part lightly waves at everyone in the room including me but tellingly he avoids waving at Mia. Mia yells, "How's the Oxford house treating you? Or whatever *sober* house you're in?" When she says this Mia has a goofy smile plastered on her face and seems fully aware of how insulting she's being. "What did you just say?" Ricky says, nervously looking at the other people in the room, paranoid now that others know he's supposed to be sober. Mia doubles down and says, "The clean and sober housing. To stay there aren't you supposed to be sober?" Ricky takes two steps toward Mia after she says this and hulks over her like he's poised to attack, at which point I lift my hand up to gesture at him to back down. He yells, "Say it to my face, you fucking bitch!" at which point Zeke tells Ricky to have a seat on the couch across the room, an instruction Ricky only reluctantly complies with. After he sits down he yells, "Don't talk to me and don't say my name!" apparently still angry with Mia for having provoked him. I'm curious about the origin of the discord, wondering whether in fact Ricky is transphobic, or whether Mia is partly responsible for playing the role of provocateur. In my peripheral vision I see Ricky animatedly talk to Zeke, this animation I think being due to Ricky's likely consumption of meth. Mia for her part is whispering to people on our side of the room, telling them that Ricky's dangerous, has no control over his anger, etc. Her endgame is clear which is to say she wants Ricky 86'd from Zeke's, an eventuality I find unlikely given that Mia was once 86'd herself. This latter piece of information was supplied to me yesterday by Butch although admittedly he didn't know any details about the banishment. Fifteen minutes later and Mia's gone and I've done another massive line of coke at which point I feel inspired to engage in conflict resolution. I sit next to Ricky on the couch and after a pause in his conversation I tap the man on the arm in order to get his attention. However before I can say a word the man asks me how many women I've slept with over the course of my entire life. I say, "Fifty to sixty. I'm not sure. I slept with a lot in my late twenties to early thirties." Ricky rocks back and forth and seems to be brimming with energy and what I see now is that he has a meth pipe in his hands. He says, "Pathetic, bro. Pathetic. I've been with 250 and I remember every single one. I even fucked twin sisters. Sisters! Hell yeah, bro! Hell yeah!" I make eye contact with Zeke after Ricky says this and we both raise our eyebrows at the lunacy of the comment and it is lunacy because I know Ricky spent a decade in prison. Ricky then proceeds to bloviate, only stopping to take the occasional hit of meth, and throughout his diatribe I wait for my chance to mention Mia. Eventually I get it and say, "By the way, sorry all that happened with Mia. What's the story? It seems like you two have some kind of beef." Ricky shakes his head, seemingly disinclined to get into any level of detail. He says, "She's just a cunt. There's nothing to know. You met one, you met them all, know what I mean?"

"My mother was murdered," Courtney says after she accepts the mirror from me that has a line and while she does the line I process what she's said. "I'm so sorry," I eventually say and elect to say nothing else, as I don't want to push her to say more if she doesn't want to pursue the topic. We're alone in Zeke's living room, as Zeke is running some sort of errand, which means that I could be twiddling my thumbs waiting for my 8-ball for upwards of an hour. Courtney then continues, "She was a drug addict and she was hitchhiking. To this day, they've never found the killer." "How old were you?" I say, carefully gauging Courtney's emotional state, as I don't want the woman to get in any way overwhelmed. Predictably however given the emotionally inoculating power of cocaine Courtney doesn't seem overwhelmed at all. She says, "I was twelve, I think. Twelve or I don't know maybe thirteen. At the time I was living with my grandparents because like I said my mom was a junkie." I reflexively say, "Right. Makes sense," after which I silently berate myself, as I think there's a dismissive element to the comment I've made. Not knowing what else to do I gesture for Courtney to hand the mirror back to me and after she does I say, "Thanks for talking to me. I'll cut us up a couple more lines." I then retrieve my baggie of blow from my breast pocket and dump a sizable quantity onto the mirror and in my eagerness to do more I forget to show verbal restraint. I say, "That's obviously a massive trauma. How do you think it impacted the course of your life?" Without missing a beat Courtney says, "Well I'm doing hard drugs as we speak. And I just got out of a relationship where I was a victim of domestic violence. Plus I've had an eating disorder for most of my life. So yeah. I'd say it's had a pretty big fucking impact." Courtney's tone is calm and detached which functions to set me at ease which is strange because her words are intensely confrontational. I then say, "Yeah that's a lot. Have you ever seen a therapist or psychiatrist? Or I don't know. Some other mental health professional?" Courtney rolls her eyes upon hearing this and leans back in her beanbag chair and when she speaks again her tone is slightly elevated. She says, "Why? So they can dope me up? So I can be on meds that make me fat and never want to have sex? No thank you. I'll stick to ketamine and coke." I say, "I get it. Meds aren't the answer for everyone. I've met plenty of people though who really do say they help." There's another pause in the conversation during which time I use a razor blade to chop up the blow, after which I again pass the mirror to Courtney. I then say, "It must be hard to have closure. Knowing the killer's still out there, I mean." Courtney then takes the line I've cut for her and reflexively coughs when she's finished and when I look at her eyes I see that they're watering. I'm guessing the latter is a response to cocaine but it occurs to me that my question may have left her emotional, the possibility of which makes me want to tread lightly. She says, "Yeah I guess. I think it was harder for my grandma and grandpa. I actually only talked to them about it once, when I was twenty." "Oh yeah?" I say at this point, accepting the mirror back from Courtney, and after she heavily sighs I sense she's poised to finally open up. It's at this moment however that Zeke opens the door to the apartment and after sensing a latent heaviness he asks us what we've been talking about. "Lots of different things," I nervously say, at which point Courtney stares at the floor. She then says, "Nothing important. I can't even remember, to be honest."

The first time I sit down with Fernando he says, "I see bullets, knives, and spirits," as if he regards this as the most essential piece of information about himself. He's Dominican and handsome and rocks back and forth in his chair, as if he were autistic which in fact for all I know he is. I ask, "Is there anything else you think I should know?" at which point Fernando dumbly smiles and then shakes his head, seemingly content with the information he's provided. I talk to the man for five more minutes but to his mind he's supplied the only data that's important and it's only when he's preparing to leave that he elaborates on his hallucinations. He says, "The knives and bullets pierce my skin. I'm being cut into pieces even though I'm alive. And the spirits are like shadows that walk around in the middle of the day." I ask him about his pharmacological history and learn that he's been on every antipsychotic known to man—including heavy-hitters like Zyprexa and Clozaril—and also learn that the meds have made no dent whatsoever in his symptoms. "Some people are just cursed," my office-mate, Debbie, says after Fernando leaves the room. And she's right. It's just above my paygrade to know who the cursed people actually are.

One night while reading a book I see a mouse skitter along the floorboards of my New York hovel, a skittering that revolts me and prompts me to research what kinds of mouse traps are available. I end up buying a trap of the "humane" variety which sadly isn't at all effective at capturing the mouse and meanwhile each day I get more revolted due to sightings of the rodent. Eventually I purchase the mouse traps that are in cartoons, the ones that function by snapping the backs of rodents, and within forty-eight hours I've successfully killed the noisome mouse. The experience however disgusts me as the dead mouse appears grotesquely disfigured in the trap and though it's undoubtedly projection I observe horror in its tiny glass-like oblivion-heavy eyes. In an unfortunate development a few days later another noisome mouse presents itself in my peripheral vision and when it does so I commit to using a different kind of trap. Ultimately I elect for glue traps, one of which is successful in securing the offending mouse, a fact I become aware of when one night after opening the door to my apartment I turn on the light and hear a hideous sound. The sound is equidistantly perched between a whine and a screech and though it isn't especially loud it's loud enough to give me goosebumps. As I approach the glue trap I see a small mouse trying desperately to escape, flailing its body but only getting more mired in the glue as it does so. "That's like me," I say aloud, uncertain of precisely what I mean, but having enough of a general idea to be placed in a negative cast of mind. As I stand above the flailing being it occurs to me that up until now I hadn't considered the endgame with the glue-trapped mouse, an endgame that it would seem involves throwing a still-living creature in the trash. "And then what?" I ask. "It just starves to death?" The prospect of this sickens me and strikes me as much more inhumane even than the cartoon-trap, the realization of which fact makes me determined to liberate the mouse. I then retrieve a spoon and pick up the trap, all the while doing my best to not attend to the squirming mouse, and thereafter I take the mouse out to the stairwell of my dorm. At this point I seat myself on one of the stairs and use the spoon to help the mouse escape the trap, a feat I accomplish but that immediately darkens my mood. The reason for this darkening is that after I liberate the mouse from the glue trap it leaps off the sixth-floor stairwell to its death. I shake my head at the development and say, "At least I tried to help," not knowing that that's my problem: I'm too weak to let a dying creature die.

"I think we should break up," I say to Deborah, my girlfriend, and my heart sinks when she adopts a look of despair. "Why?" Deborah asks, seeming utterly taken aback by my words, a scenario I feared but naively hoped would not obtain. I want to be as truthful as I can be while also being considerate of Deborah's feelings, a tightrope I'm doing all that I can do to walk. I say, "I just don't see us together long term. You're a wonderful person, Deborah, and you deserve someone who's totally committed to you." Deborah looks simultaneously hurt and disbelieving and she kindly calls bullshit on what I'm saying, asking me, "Tell me the truth: why don't you want to be with me?" At that moment I look at Deborah and am overwhelmed by the urge to have sex, to such a degree that I feel myself develop an erection. This strikes me as disgusting and uncouth and in an attempt to detumesce I conjure up the image of my father naked, a strategy that within seconds proves to be successful. I say, "I just want to break up. This isn't working, Deborah. It's not working for me, and that should be enough." "No," Deborah says as she steels up her resolve. "I've been good to you so you owe me the truth." I consider the merit of what she's said and after sighing I commit to telling Deborah the unvarnished truth which is to say I intend to speak honestly, without fear of how my words are going to land. I then close my eyes and say, "I was never that attracted to you, Deborah. You were just a rebound from my relationship with Zoe," at which point I open my eyes and observe unmitigated horror. She then says, "That's the cruelest thing anyone's ever said to me," and I instantly see the lesson imparted by the moment: never be fully honest with people. They don't want it and neither do you.

There's a new addition to the Zen center, a balding guy in his late twenties or early thirties, and the guy, Aaron, and I hit it off immediately. He has a ribald sense of humor and is quick to laugh and is relaxed and I can tell he also takes a liking to me. Aaron's from Austin, Texas, and tells me he dealt cocaine while he was there and that furthermore while doing so he "did bad things," a comment that alarms me. Nevertheless we bond about books and music and Zen and one day while we're chopping wood he tells me why he cares about me and why he feels like we're connected. He says, "You remind me a lot of my brother. Sometimes when I talk to you I forget that I'm not talking to him." I then tell him that that's flattering and ask him if he's close with his brother now, to which Aaron says, "He shot himself nine years ago. So I don't know. 'Close' is a bit of a stretch."

For Peyton's thirtieth birthday I arrange to get twenty pills of MDMA which on the night of her party I place in an ashtray on the living room table. The pills are available to everyone but only four of us partake, with Peyton and Larry taking two, Brad taking one, and me taking three due to my reduced sensitivity to serotonergic drugs. Brad, who supplied the ecstasy, also brings cocaine to the party and by 8 PM I've already done several lines. Ambient music plays and the vibe at the party is relaxed yet festive and most importantly Peyton's spirits seem to be high. However though the cocaine and ecstasy feel good I'm still not as high as I want to be and ninety minutes in I take two more ecstasy pills. An hour after that I take more MDMA which adds up to seven pills in one hundred and fifty minutes, a staggering quantity that I handle surprisingly well. At the tail end of the party Jeff—a fiction writer who specializes in writing about young millennials experiencing ennui—begins hitting on a poet in the program, Rebecca. They've slept together once before but Jeff had no interest in pursuing a relationship as he's long been fixated on another writer in the program, Kelly. In my expansive and magnanimous state I encourage Rebecca and Jeff to each take an ecstasy pill and after conferring with each other they agree to take half a pill each. An hour later they leave together and before they do so I tell Rebecca not to sleep with Jeff, as he clearly doesn't want to date her and is smitten with Kelly. Rebecca's dismissive of what I say, claiming that she's a grown woman who can do exactly what she wants, and as they enter Jeff's car I feel remorse for having encouraged their use of drugs. The following day I learn that Jeff and Rebecca did have sex at Jeff's apartment and after asking Rebecca how she feels about it she says she doesn't know. Soon thereafter Jeff puts the kibosh on any potential relationship with Rebecca which leads her to describe Jeff to others as a predatory rapist. When asked to detail the sequence of events Rebecca describes a coercive encounter, one in which Jeff digitally penetrated her as she expressed uncertainty about intercourse. What's most upsetting to Rebecca however is that Jeff lied about how open he was to entering into a romantic relationship, an openness Rebecca is certain was never actually there. Rebecca conceives of this duplicity as rape, as a violation of her conditional consent, and months after the event she consults the Title IX investigator to see what recourse she has. Throughout this entire period I try to be a good friend to Rebecca, even while I balk at the idea that Jeff's behavior is anywhere close to rape. Six months after their entanglement and I'm on the Alyene house's back porch smoking a cigarette and Rebecca and I are each reclining on lawn chairs as she vents. She says, "Why can't you just call it rape? You'd never do something like that." I say, "Not now I wouldn't. But I've been in exactly Jeff's position. I've sweet-talked a woman in order to get laid." Rebecca then sits up in the lawn chair, clearly distressed by what I've said, and asks me, "You've told women you would date them, knowing full well you wouldn't, just so that you could get off?" I solemnly nod, after which Rebecca again reclines back into the lawn chair, and after sighing says, "That's too bad. Because that means you're a rapist, too."

"It's good to see you, Mike," Zoe says after we each order a cocktail at Rock Box, a karaoke bar, and after we cheers we go outside and sit at a table. We haven't seen each other in two years and she provides an efficient update as to what's occurred, an update that involves her both having a nervous breakdown and experiencing tremendous professional success. I've just completed the first year of my MFA but I talk minimally about writing as my primary objective is going back to Zoe's apartment and having sex with her there. We get drunk and sing songs and eventually walk over to Zoe's Capitol Hill apartment, at which point Zoe regales me with her rendition of a Decemberists' song, a band I absolutely loathe. "It's amazing you learned to play guitar," I say, to which she says, "That's not the only thing I've learned," a comment that baffles me but that seems to contain innuendo. Zoe then puts down her guitar and leads the way to her bedroom, at which point we lie on her bed and begin to kiss each other. We do so for maybe a minute, at which point Zoe excuses herself to the restroom, a clear sign to me that Zoe is preparing to have sex. Consequently I take off my clothes and sprawl out naked on the bed, the fact of which horrifies Zoe when she reenters the room. "What in the hell are you doing?" Zoe asks as she points at my genitalia and the truth is that I struggle with how to competently answer her question. I say, "You're upset? Zoe, I thought you wanted to have sex," a thought Zoe calls out as "presumptuous," "pathetic," and "kind of rapey." I then roll off the bed and put on my clothes as quickly as I can, during which time Zoe repeatedly shakes her head and mutters, "I can't believe this is happening." Zoe then escorts me to her front door where my intention is to ask for her forgiveness but not before I contextualize my behavior. I say, "We were making out and also have an extensive sexual history. So you can see why I thought what I did." Zoe narrows her eyes, clearly not at all receptive to what I've said, and I briefly observe a sadistic glint in her eyes. She says, "You're becoming your father. You're going to end up exactly like him," at which point she nods peremptorily and closes her door. I then turn around and walk back toward Rock Box, where I intend to get extremely drunk, and as I do so I have the thought, "There's no escape. There's no escape and you know it."

"I don't understand," Selene says as Adam explains the premise of the exhibit, this even though he's being very clear in his explanation. I say, "I think what Adam's saying is that there are pictures of Holocaust victims that PETA is juxtaposing with images of animals being slaughtered." Selene clenches her fists and yells, "What the fuck, Adam!" at which point I gesture with my hand for her to calm down. I say, "No need to shoot the messenger. Just because Adam is a vegan doesn't mean he approves of everything PETA does." Meanwhile Adam shrugs his shoulders, seemingly unaffected by Selene's hostility, and when he speaks again it's clear he's not afraid of confrontation. He says, "I don't know, Selene. Factory farming is evil. Pissing people off is worth it if it gets animals to stop being butchered." Selene narrows her eyes and jabs her right index finger toward Adam, at which point she says, "That you're defending this, Adam, makes you fucking evil." Adam cackles and points at the sandwich in her hand and then says, "The turkey in your sandwich was once an animal that could love and think and feel." Selene then looks at me and says, "Fuck this. Whose side are you on, Michael?" after which Adam looks at me and says, "Yeah, who's the asshole in this situation?" I look first at one and then the other, bewildered how two extreme liberals could come to hate each other, and say, "There's no hope for us. Every one of us is doomed."

"I gave my life awayyy!" I sing at the end of my rendition of "Under the Bridge," the karaoke song I'm currently singing at a bar in San Antonio. I'm in the city for AWP, the decadent and depraved writer's conference, although as I complete the song I think, "This AWP hasn't been all that depraved." I think this to myself though earlier tonight I did a decent amount of coke, as I have each of the preceding two nights I've been in San Antonio. Still for whatever reason it doesn't feel like I'm engaging in debauchery, presumably because at this conference I'm not on the prowl to get laid. At every other AWP I've gone to I've been single and hungry and consequently delectated in the pleasures of the flesh with acquaintances, if not total strangers. However at this AWP I'm with my fiancée,

Peyton, and though we have an open relationship I'm not looking to sow my wild oats. I'm extremely happy with Peyton or so I tell myself in the present moment, though admittedly I'll evaluate the matter very differently once I commit to sobriety. I hand the mic back to the KJ who calls up the next singer—Autumn, singing "Everybody" by the Backstreet Boys—at which point I focus on what's of immediate importance which is to say procuring more cocaine. I brought an 8-ball to the conference but between Peyton and me and our honky-tonk Texan roommate, Buster, we consumed the entire 8-ball in two and a half days. (At this stage of my addiction this seems like a lot.) This poses a definite problem as I don't want to be sober at all nor in fact as a solution am I content with just getting drunk. I say this because an hour ago I saw a man flirting with Peyton while she was smoking and in her eyes and face I could see how turned on she was. If I drink tonight without doing blow I'll in all likelihood get depressed which is to say I'll emotionally shut down and be incapable of connecting with Peyton. All of which is to say it's imperative that I obtain more cocaine which admittedly is risky because I don't have any plugs—let alone trustworthy plugs—in San Antonio. In a fit of desperation I survey the crowd at the bar and ask myself which person among them is most likely to have cocaine. I settle on a portly and jovial-looking Latino guy who's socializing with other Latinos who together as a group have commandeered the back of the bar. I try to approach the man with confidence but I imagine I cut a ridiculous figure as I'm a fat Northwesterner sporting flannel and an unruly mop of hair. "Hey man, could I talk to you for a second?" I say to the guy and he furrows his brow, evidently confused as to why I'd be approaching him when he's with his friends. Fortunately however given how dweebish I undoubtedly look the man doesn't feel threatened by my presence and even takes a few steps aside so that we can have some privacy. "Whachu lookin for?" he says abruptly, clearly not looking to waste any time making small talk, and as I look into his appraising eyes I tell him I'm looking for cocaine. He says nothing for several seconds, clearly attempting to determine whether I'm deserving of his trust, and in his nervousness he asks to see my ID. "My ID?" I ask, clearly confused, at which point he exhibits a hint of frustration. He says, "I want to make sure you're not a cop, bro. Show me your ID or no deal." I retrieve my wallet and do as I'm told and meanwhile tell him I'm in town for a conference, the latter of which piece of information he expresses no interest in whatsoever. He says, "I have to call a guy to bring it over. So you need to make it worth his while. At least $200 worth. That gonna work?" I avidly nod, clearly excited, as this means I won't be overwhelmed by the image of Peyton getting turned on by the guy who talked to her while she smoked, or at least that I'll be able to cope with it enough that I can still emotionally connect with Peyton later. Over the last year of doing cocaine this is the precedent I've set by which I mean I use the drug to escape the feelings of helplessness and fear that the open relationship has elicited. In fact since discovering coke at thirty-five my experiences have followed a predictable template which is to say that regardless of who I'm talking to within minutes of doing my second line I'll start talking about how difficult it is for me to be in my relationship. Of course I also emphasize the love I have for Peyton and how committed I am to making her happy but once I'm speeding at some point I'm going to talk about my sadness and abjection. Learning that cocaine is on the way has already done wonders to alleviate my anxiety and as I sit at a table in the bar with other conference attendees from my university I impatiently wait for the man to get me drugs. Forty-five minutes pass during which time I hear all manner of karaoke standards—"Don't Stop Believin'," "Wonderwall," "Say It Ain't So," etc.—but after hearing an especially grievous rendition of "Rocket Man" my anxiety again starts to build. I text the Latino dealer, paranoid that I've been ripped off for $200, and seconds later the man responds simply, with "just chill." I then go outside to smoke a cigarette and talk to Peyton who looks haggard from the past days' partying and after I reach her I update her about the status of the drugs. She says, "Do we really need to party tonight? All we've done at this conference is do drugs." I ignore the criticism embedded in the comment and instead simply state how soon the drugs are poised to arrive although my uninformed estimate—five minutes—proves to be totally wrong. I don't receive a follow-up text for almost an hour and when I do it simply says, "Go to the bathroom," which irritates me but nevertheless I do as I'm told. I see my guy immediately after I open the door as he's standing next to the sink and the sink is directly adjacent to the door. He then says, "Sorry. I can't help you," at which point he nervously darts his eyes, and as he does so I feel a surge of anger in my body. I say, "What in the fuck? I gave you $200, man," after which the hefty man widens his eyes and looks in the direction of the sink. He again says, "Sorry. Can't help you," and again gestures with his eyes toward the sink, at the completion of which gesture I finally understand what the man is trying to do. I scour the sink area with my eyes and eventually locate the bag of powder, at which point I palm it and wish the man well. Twenty minutes later Peyton and I are in the hotel room doing lines and unsurprisingly I feel totally rejuvenated. Peyton seems to feel this way as well, as indicated by how much she's begun to talk, so much so in fact that I'm finding it difficult to get in a word edgewise. I appreciate this development as I tend to hold forth when I'm doing coke and to furthermore sometimes talk over Peyton when I'm flying from the drug. However it gradually becomes clear that Peyton isn't simply being extra-talkative from the coke but that she is in fact experiencing some kind of drug-induced mania. She's not psychotic and isn't hallucinating and doesn't seem to have lost contact with reality but she is frantically pacing and talking faster than I've ever seen her talk. I say, "I think this coke is cut. Maybe we shouldn't do any more lines," a suggestion that seems to irritate Peyton. Despite Peyton's look of irritation I put away the bag of coke and it's only as I'm doing so that she delivers the coup de grâce. She says, "You're in denial, Michael. At some point I'm also going to want to sleep with men." Peyton resumes pacing after she says this but tellingly doesn't stop making eye contact with me and in her eyes there's willfulness, anger, and frustration. What's astonishing about this moment is that despite the cocaine-and-meth-induced euphoria and despite the layers of denial I'm utterly lost in I know in my bones that Peyton is correct. Experimenting with an open relationship has been a nightmare, by which experimentation I mean that Peyton has intermittently slept with women whereas meanwhile during her escapades I've smoked cigarettes and listened to Nirvana's *Unplugged* record on repeat. On and off cocaine I've talked ad nauseam to people about how painful the situation is and almost everyone hearing it has told me how precarious my mental state seems to be. "But I can grow and change," is what I say. "I can learn to be okay with it." It's only at this moment—as Peyton makes eye contact with me and manically paces while we're in San Antonio for AWP—that I see what everyone else has seen: that our relationship is toxic. Toxic and doomed. This was true of course even when Peyton was only sleeping with women but if I stay in the relationship now it's going to absolutely destroy my soul. In fact that was the main parameter: when engaging in extra-curriculars Peyton would only sleep with women, the reason for which was that we were only opening up the relationship at all so that Peyton could get more in touch with the queer part of her identity. Or so Peyton insisted, just as she insisted that she still loved me and that our relationship was secure, both of which points I realize now at this very moment are totally false. The point is: I can't endure this. And if I hitch my wagon to Peyton, I'll die. And I don't want to die. Or maybe I do. But not every day. Some days I do really want to live.

"You're the angriest person I've ever met!" a manic client, Charlie, screams at me, this though I'm acting extraordinarily calm. Charlie points his shaking finger at me and looks at my coworker, Natalie, at which point he asks Natalie if she agrees with his assessment. Natalie says, "Not really, no. I've never seen Michael even yell," an observation which elicits vigorous head-shaking on the part of Charlie. He then says, "It's because of his disability," declining to elaborate any further, a cryptic comment I have no desire to follow up on whatsoever. Natalie however is curious and asks Charlie what he means by disability, at which point Charlie points in the general direction of his eyes. He says, "His glasses. His vision. You can see the rage flowing in his veins. And all just because his eyes are fucked up." Charlie's hyperventilating at this point, and his agitation's rapidly increasing, so I make the decision to exit the room. I say, "Take care of yourself, Charlie. I'll see you later, okay?" and as I walk away he screams, "No you won't! You'll be too busy fighting with God and His angels!" I'm amazed by this level of insight. I do in fact fight with God and His angels. To be honest sometimes it feels like that's all I ever do.

It's hot and it's humid even though the sun has set in Lafayette and now that I've finished my reading for the night I'm fiending for coke. I first tried the drug a year ago, mainly at the recommendation of Peyton and Brad, my mj dealer, and my initial reaction to the drug was defined by disappointment and boredom. That night I did two small-to-medium-sized lines over the course of two hours and truthfully noticed little-to-no change in either mood or cognition. In fact so underwhelmed was I by the drug that the day after I did it I told a program friend of mine, Jeff—a man who claimed to adore cocaine—that I'd likely never do it again. He shook his head after my comment and said, "That's crazy, man. You didn't do enough," a comment that two weeks later would prove to be correct. On that day, a Friday, Peyton and I threw a party at our rented house on Alyene Drive, a party that was attended by seventy-five percent of the program. Pot smoke permeated the house and countless bottles of wine and beer and etc. were consumed and everyone seemed to be in a pleasant if not euphoric state of mind. Knowing how heavily attended the party would be and how eager I was to show people a good time I secured an 8-ball from Brad that could be shared by anyone who wished to partake. This as it turned out was probably ten to twelve people, people who weren't especially covert about leaving the main room of the party to do coke in Peyton's and my bedroom. In any case what matters is that the party was the most memorable of my life, consisting as it did of me joyously hobnobbing with nearly everyone present. I hopscotched from one conversation to the next, delicate and graceful and charming, and as night turned to early morning I realized that I'd been converted into a cocaine devotee. In the weeks and months that have followed I've gone about my business writing papers, attending class, etc., but I've also done cocaine any chance I can get. The only plug I have however is Brad, someone who's wary of me developing an addiction to cocaine, and who consequently micromanages the amount of the drug I consume. Brad will rarely sell me bags, generally only when Peyton and I are throwing a party, which means that if I want to do cocaine I have to go to Brad's and do lines in his presence. I should also note that Brad smokes something like a dozen dabs per day, dabs I also take but that leave me sufficiently stupefied that I can barely talk after I take them. Compounding this sense of stupefaction are the conversations I have with Brad while we're on dabs, centering as they often do on the spirits Brad is certain walk the earth. He'll talk for example about "earth-bound" souls that haunt certain locations "for a thousand years, give or take," and he's utterly convinced that Amy Allan—from the TV show *The Dead Files*—is a medium whose commentary is as reliable as carbon-14 dating. Throughout Brad's insanity I only pay minimal attention—when it becomes necessary I'll offer a punctuating remark, such as "That's crazy," "Totally dude," or "Yeah yeah yeah"—as my mind is focused on cocaine, which Brad always seems to have around. Brad doesn't do cocaine alone nor as far as I know does he do it with any of the other customers he has which effectively means that he keeps cocaine around in order to maintain my friendship. He knows I'm slavishly devoted to the drug, that I genuflect at its altar, and that so long as I'm given at least one line every hour I'll make myself available to hear him bloviate about ghosts, aliens, Bigfoot, and the nature of the cosmos and time. Anyway on this particular night I've finished reading for school and after coordinating with Peyton I go to a bar, Caffé Cottage, with her and some program friends. I proceed to get drunk, at which point my desire for coke is uncontrollable, to such a degree that I'm prepared to ask strangers at the bar if they have any they're willing to sell. Brad refuses to sell me any as he thinks I've been doing it far too often which means that if I want coke I have to find another source. I begin by approaching Courtney, another writer in the program, who from what I gather has befriended some ne'er-do-wells in the Lafayette community. I ask her if one of these crust-punk-like friends can locate cocaine and she says she'll ask the point person, Skywalker. She does this immediately and I'm told that a friend of Skywalker's, Sean, can get me an 8-ball if I pick him up from his house. There's no doubt I'm over the legal limit but I embark on the trip immediately and thirty minutes later Sean is in my Subaru Impreza. My expectation is that he'll have the coke on him so I'm both irritated and disappointed when I learn that he has to meet up with his dealer in order to obtain the ball. Nevertheless I'm committed so I end up driving Sean to a nearby gas station where I first withdraw $300 and then wait for Sean's dealer to arrive. "That's him," Sean says. "Give me the money and I'll be back soon." After I do as I'm instructed Sean exits my vehicle and enters a black Escalade, an Escalade that promptly exits the lot. I wait ten or fifteen minutes, utterly convinced I've been fleeced, a conviction that exists in part because Sean isn't responding to my texts. I'm poised to leave the parking lot and return to Caffè Cottage alone when Sean turns the gas station corner and enters my vehicle. Sean says, "Got it. Let's go to Cottage," at which point I drive to the bar, and it's only when we pull into a parking spot there that Sean grabs me by the arm. "I have a favor to ask you," Sean says. "It's a little embarrassing, but I'm hoping you're cool with it. It's your coke though so you can say no if you want." There's vulnerability in the man's voice, as if he's concerned about being judged, and my body tenses up because I'm expecting a heavy disclosure. "Don't be embarrassed," I say. "You just did me a solid. If I can help you out, you know that I will." Sean nods in seeming gratitude and then places one of his hands in his pocket, at which point he pulls out a syringe. He says, "Do you mind if I shoot up a little of your coke? Not much. Just enough to get feeling good." Sean then looks at me expectantly, as if he's anticipating rejection. "By all means, man," I say. "Take as much as you'd like." After Sean hears this he pulls a spoon out of his pocket and also produces the ball of cocaine. He then dabs a tenth of a gram onto the spoon and combines it with water he gets from a Nalgene bottle he finds on the Subaru's floor. "Lucky me," Sean says as he points at the Nalgene bottle, after saying which he grabs the syringe to stir (and thereby dissolve) the cocaine into the water. Having dissolved the cocaine Sean retrieves a cigarette from a pack in his pocket, a cigarette he throws out of the passenger-side window after he takes out its filter. He then uses the filter to extract the solution from the spoon, at which point he commences looking for a vein. I'm transfixed throughout this whole process, as if I'm rubbernecking at the sight of a totaled car on the highway, and it's only when Sean starts poking around his arm that I begin to get squeamish. By poking I mean that Sean inserts the needle into his arm several times, after each of which insertions he says some variation of, "Nope. Not good enough." After one final insertion Sean says, "Jackpot," and injects the solution, at which point he closes his eyes and seems to luxuriate in whatever blissed out feeling he's feeling. I say, "I've only snorted coke. What does it feel like when you shoot up?" Sean opens his eyes and looks alert and has a smile on his face and it's clear to me that he's about to deliver a capping line. "It's like diving into a warm pool," he says. "Once you shoot up there's no going back." Sean then puts away his paraphernalia and exits the car, leaving me alone in the near-dark of my Subaru, and I can only shake my head at what I've just witnessed. "There's no going back," I repeat. And Sean's right. There is no going back. The question is: knowing what I know now would I really even want to?

I'm staring out of the windshield of my janky 1986 blue Toyota Camry while I'm in the parking lot attached to Seattle's Greenlake park. I'm with Ellen, a girl I met at a local high school debate tournament, and the air is thick with some holy mixture of fear, shame, longing, and lust. There's never been any sexual contact between us nor in fact have I ever had any sexual contact with anyone and the truth is that I'm scared shitless of what we both know lies ahead. I want to consume Ellen, to destroy her, but to do so in the most delicate way, and the seeming impossibility of doing this leaves me paralyzed and only capable of looking out at the distant water. From this vantage it looks like blackened glass and I imagine the vast world submerged under its placid exterior and I make a mental note of the parallels to the present moment. "Michael," Ellen says, an action which prompts me to turn my head, and after I do so I observe something in her eyes that emboldens me. What is it that I see? I see myself in the mirror which is to say I see a scared shitless creature who both desires another creature and feels the fear of rejection. I lean forward and kiss her and soon my hand is on her breast above her clothing and we fumble awkwardly at each other across the chasm of our seats. Ellen asks, "Should we move to the back of the car?" and I immediately pull back and exit the vehicle, at which point Ellen steps out of the car and opens the rear passenger side door. Soon the doors are all closed and I feel like I'm lunging toward the woman which I'm not but in my desperation I feel like every movement of mine is suffused with a kind of lustful fury. In actuality I'm restrained or at least to a sufficient degree that Ellen has to instigate much of the sexual contact, most notably in her drawing my hand downward toward her vagina. I have no idea what I'm doing and don't rub her clitoris at all, all I do is digitally penetrate her for some indefinite period. The moment feels sacred, almost holy, and I'm certain this is rooted in my desperation to transcend myself, a desperation that yearns for Ellen but also yearns to escape the confines of my body. That is to say my overwhelming desire for Ellen has made me more acutely aware of the distance that exists between me and other human beings. After our abortive and adolescent union I drive Ellen back to her house and throughout the car ride we're silent but silent in a contented kind of way. We kiss when we say goodbye and I then slowly drive away and en route to my house I repeatedly smell my fingers. "I've been branded," I say out loud, thinking of myself as a pig or cow, some piece of livestock. Which I am, basically. We're just animals, you and I.

The apartment when I enter is exceptionally clean which is surprising given what my supervisor told me about Sally. "She's got a sob story, for sure," Misty, my boss, told me before I drove over to Sally's apartment, and based on this I assumed Sally's apartment would be in disarray. I introduce myself to Sally, explaining that I'm a new social worker with the mental health agency that serves her, Navos, and ask her if there's anything she wants to know about me. Sally's blandly cheerful and shrugs but I sense there's a void lurking just beneath the surface, a void which experience tells me Sally's likely eager to share. "Okay," I say. "What about you? Is there anything about you or your story that you'd like me to know?" Sally thrums the fingers of her left hand against the table we're sitting at and then asks me if I know anything about classical music. I say, "Unfortunately, no. I wish I knew more. I take it you're a fan of classical music?" Sally stops thrumming her fingers and lifts up her hand to examine it and as she does so she says, "These are the fingers of a once-astonishingly gifted pianist." I nod, impressed, and ask Sally if she still has any occasion to play, after which question Sally glares at me like I've said something deeply inappropriate. She then points at a Ziploc bag, one that's at the far edge of the table, and asks me if I know what's inside that bag. I say, "Photos, it looks like. Lots and lots of photos. I can't make them out, but I can tell there are a lot." "Anything else?" Sally says, encouraging me to take a second look, and when I do I see the edge of an orange medicine bottle. I say, "Some medication, it looks like. Your psych meds, maybe? I don't know. I can't really tell." Sally says, "Nineteen years ago I performed at a concert not knowing that an hour before my husband and son had been killed in a car crash. I performed incredibly. Brilliantly. And I did it all while my husband and son's bodies were mangled. I haven't performed in public a single time since the time of their deaths." I say nothing in response to this, allowing the moment to breathe, and before long Sally again points at the bag. She says, "Do you know what I call that bag?" a question to which I shake my head in response, after which point she says, "My suicide kit." I feel my pulse quicken and feel my breathing get shallow, as the reference to suicide immediately calls to mind Bob. I say, "Why do you call it that?" after which Sally looks at me with a twinkle in her eye before she reaches across the table and retrieves the Ziploc with her hands. She holds it up to eye level and looks first at the bag and then at me and then says, "There's enough medication in here to kill me. If I decide to die, it will be with the drugs in this bag. I reserve that option for myself one day a week." Horrified, and confused, I ask, "One day per week? Are you saying there's only one day that you feel suicidal?" Sally chuckles and shakes her head, likely amazed by my stupidity, and then says, "I want to die all the time. But I only allow myself to look at their photos one day per week. And each time I look at the photos I decide if this is the week that I want to end it all." "I see," I say, not knowing how else to respond to what Sally's said, and suddenly I'm anxious about the viability of the career path I've chosen. "Son. How do you feel?" Sally suddenly asks as she examines the undoubtedly terrified look on my face and it's clear to me that everything that's transpiring is a test. Sally wants to determine whether I'm an acceptable container for her grief, whether I'm capable of safely absorbing the agony that defines her waking life. And the truth is: I'm not. I'm not up to the challenge. And I don't want to bullshit the woman, so before leaving her apartment—and subsequently resigning from my job—I decide to tell her one thing that's true. I say, "My heart hurts for you, Sally," but sadly even this is misleading, as while my heart does hurt it isn't in the service of anyone or anything greater than myself. Not Sally. Not Bob. Not God. Not art. My heart just hurts. Period. Full stop. End of story.

I examine the cocaine I've poured on top of the toilet paper dispenser and then mutter to myself, "A little more isn't going to hurt anybody." It's my third day of work and in five minutes I'm due to co-facilitate a group therapy session with homeless clients, the topic of which group I was just told was substance abuse. I acknowledge to myself the hypocrisy of my behavior—of all people, who am I to give advice on how to cope with substance abuse?—but at this stage in my addiction I'm capable of the most extraordinary mental gymnastics. That is to say while I dimly apprehend the truth—of my addiction, of my hypocrisy, etc.—I'm constitutionally incapable of dwelling in that apprehension. The means by which I escape this apprehension is through the escalating algebra of my need which is to say I escape it by my all-consuming obsession with drugs. Like everyone else of course thoughts flit about my brain throughout the day but it all exists against the backdrop of a larger question: when am I going to do my next line? I then add another tenth of a gram to the line and snort it using a rolled-up dollar bill and then wipe my finger across the top of the metal dispenser. The residual cocaine is now on my finger and I rub it across my bottom gums and after flushing the toilet I exit the stall and look at myself in the mirror. I'm concerned about being found out so I tilt my head back and examine my nostril, this in order to determine whether any powdery remnants will be visible to those who come into contact with me. And then at that moment I feel the light bulb turn on and after staring at my eyebags I clap my hands together and yell, "Let the healing begin!"

The alarm on my phone has just gone off which means I've been asleep for eighty minutes, eighty minutes being the maximum amount of time I can permit myself to close my eyes. I'm hungover again as I am every morning that I work and because I was at a club until closing time last night I've only gotten four hours of sleep. The combination of the lack of sleep and the hangover has rendered me professionally useless and although on my written schedule I'm going to claim to have spent half an hour with each of my organization's clients, I only spent a combined ten minutes with the three located in this facility. I'm grateful for this of course because it means I can sleep during my shift and in fact most days this is how I catch up on sleep. That is to say I regularly lie about how long I spent with each of my organization, Navos', clients, all of whom either live in their homes or in retirement communities. Unlike other social work jobs I've had the clientele here aren't populated with the floridly psychotic but instead mostly with people struggling with intractable depression. My job is mindless, almost robotic, and involves me subjecting clients to a battery of questions, all of which are aimed at assessing suicide risk and ensuring medication compliance. I'm able to perform these tasks quickly which means that were I so inclined—and I *am* so inclined—I could exploit the trusting nature of my boss and of the entire organization. As I lift up my driver's seat from the reclining position it was in I look at my haggard eyes in the rearview mirror. "You're not an ethical person," I say to myself as I experience a twinge of remorse for exploiting others, although the moment soon passes and before long I've shut my eyes to get another ten minutes of rest.

I arrange to take LSD with Noah and Bill, LSD I'll obtain from Brad and then bring on an airplane to Santa Barbara.

The plan goes off without a hitch and soon I'm walking barefoot on the beach with my two best friends, neither of whom has ever taken the drug. I give them each one piece of blotter whereas I take three pieces of blotter, this because my antipsychotic makes me substantially less responsive to the effects of psychedelics. Bill comes up seemingly immediately and spends forty-five minutes groaning on the sand, a development that leaves Noah irritated and me feeling concerned. I say, "It'll be fine, Bill. Let go. You can't control what happens during the trip," a platitude delivered curtly but that inexplicably works. Soon Bill has stood up and is walking with the two of us on the beach at which point soon thereafter Noah comes up and his legs become wobbly. He proposes we sit in the shade of a palm tree which Bill and I agree to and soon we're each lying down saying nothing and hallucinating. It's clear to me however that I'm the least impaired of the three of us, a fact that doesn't surprise me but is nevertheless disappointing. We each then stare at the sky and talk about sensations blooming inside us and generally are marooned inside our own skulls. Meanwhile I'm thinking about Peyton and our relationship as she's recently begun to sleep with other people and for my part the acid makes me see how uncomfortable I am with this open element. I open my mouth to discuss this, to expunge the pain from my soul, but realize that to speak about it right now would bring negative energy to the trip. Soon we've giggled and peaked and rolled about mindlessly on the sand after which point I feel an afterglow and hours later sleep as soundly as I ever have. The next day we go hiking which I was under the impression would be easy but midway to our destination I sit down and say

I can't go any farther. Bill and Noah sit down too and the three of us debrief about our relationships, a debrief I begin by discussing the pain I didn't discuss the previous day. Little advice is given to me, as Bill and Noah have shared their opinions with me many times, the gist of which opinions are that my relationship is irredeemably toxic. Knowing their opinions on the matter and having met my goal of expressing my pain we move to Noah who volunteers very little. Bill then discusses his relationship with AJ, his girlfriend, which involves an analysis of their anemic-sounding sex life, and in the process of doing so he confesses to being bisexual. "What do you mean you're bisexual?" Noah asks, baffled by the development, as Bill is thirty-five and has given no previous indication of such an inclination. We delve deeper into Bill's desires and learn that he watches gay pornography and that furthermore when he watches it he imagines being a bottom. "Yeah, that's pretty gay," Noah says which prompts both Bill and me to laugh although after Bill's confession my mind turns to my childhood rape. I talk to my friends and say that in another world I too am bisexual or at the very least I experimented with men while I was in college. I explain that while I minimize it when it comes up being raped as a child has had lingering after-effects, including me experiencing discomfort when I'm hit on by gay men. I'm also averse to anal penetration, a fact I've learned over the course of my sexual life when at different times women have stuck a finger in my ass as they were fellating me. Bill says, "It's not too late to mess around. And it might even be healing," which is a thought I've had before and that a former sexual partner also suggested. "It's too late for me," I say. "There's no undoing the damage that's been done." Bill then shrugs his shoulders and says, "That's only true because you've told yourself it is." The following morning before my flight I stick a finger in my ass as I take a shower and it feels sufficiently good that I masturbate to completion. However when I take out my finger I see a hint of feces on my cuticle and as I wash it off with soap I mutter, "See? That's what you fucking get."

I'm in Bill's apartment and we've each taken our final lines, two minutes after which I entertain an addict-like idea. I say, "Let's take the other gram from Noah. We can replace it tomorrow when you call your guy," and after I say this Bill skeptically narrows his eyes. He says, "You want to steal Noah's coke? That would be really shitty of us, don't you think?" I shake my head and make a dismissive gesture with my hands, as if Bill were intellectually subnormal and having a hard time keeping up. I say, "It won't be a problem. You'll just call your guy tomorrow night, and we'll replace the gram before Noah even knows it." Bill shrugs his shoulders after my comment, after which he points his finger at me and says, "If there's fallout from any of this, you have to take responsibility. This isn't my idea. It's yours, and I want you to acknowledge that." I acknowledge the point and then walk to Noah's apartment whereupon after using a spare key to enter it I observe the man sleeping. I open a drawer in Noah's dresser and palm the gram he purchased mere hours earlier and my mind is a void as I tiptoe out of his apartment. I then return to Bill's apartment where the two of us proceed to quickly do the entire gram, after which I return to Noah's apartment in order to sleep. The following morning Noah discovers that his cocaine is gone which elicits first bafflement and secondly an extraordinary amount of anger. "This is all Bill," Noah says. "It's got Bill written all over it." For my part I disconfirm nothing, neither nodding nor shaking my head, and I do my best to weather the storm that is Noah ranting. At some point post-rant Noah acknowledges my complicity in the debacle and asks me, "Why would you go along with his bullshit?" I then look away from Noah and say the only remotely true thing I can think of, which is: "Some people are just really persuasive."

Sarah hands me a pipe as Peyton and I enter her apartment and says, "Time to celebrate, bitches!" It's the night of the election in 2016 and the atmosphere in the apartment is overwhelmingly festive. People are laughing and swaying and giving each other hugs, this even though the first results haven't yet come in. Peyton and I take several hits and then each grab a beer and before long we're swept up in the air of celebration. Soon the first returns are announced and it's clear Hillary isn't doing all that well and suddenly I have an intuition of darkness. "Don't worry, guys," Sarah says after taking a hit. "FiveThirtyEight said Hilary was eighty percent to win." A fellow student, Nolan, then says, "As far as odds go, twenty percent isn't all that low." Sarah shakes her head dismissively and starts to pack another bowl and then says, "I have a friend that's a politico. This thing is in the bag." Meanwhile I experience a surge in anxiety, to such a large degree in fact that I lie down on Sarah's living room carpet in the middle of the party. My eyes are closed for the next two hours and I envision what America will be like under

Trump and with the exception of Peyton occasionally checking in on me it's like I'm not even really here. Eventually I stand up and tell Peyton I want to leave, a sentiment that seems to be shared by most of the people at the party. I hug half a dozen people goodbye and to each one utter some banality meant to comfort—"It will all be okay," "We'll get through this," etc.—but we all know that some events are just horrible and that there is no real silver lining. When we return to our apartment I bloviate about how nightmarish a Trump presidency is going to be and eventually Peyton, clearly irritated, makes a high-level critique. She says, "You're a straight white cis male. You're not going to be affected by Trump at all. So why are you acting all upset about it, like you're the one who's in danger?" I say, "Point taken. Or at least kind of. But if people I love are affected, then I'm affected. It's not like human beings only care about themselves." Peyton walks over to our balcony, at which point she closes the door and lights up a cigarette, an action which effectively ends the conversation. But before she does so Peyton looks at me sadly and says, "When it's just the two of us you don't need to pretend."

I'm three blocks from my house in Capitol Hill when I begin to hear the manic cawing of a crow, a cawing that gets increasingly annoying as I approach the power line it's on. "Stupid fucking animal," I mutter as I pass under the crow, at which point I see the cause of the crow's distress. There's a dead crow on the sidewalk and though of course I can't know this with any certainty it seems clear to me that the dead crow is being mourned by the crow on the powerline. After I recognize this a great deal goes through my mind including the thought that if grief isn't unique to humanity then what exactly is? High-level math obviously isn't being performed by dolphins or elephants or chimps but from what I gather grief and language aren't the sole purview of humans either. I mutter, "We're not special. We're just like them," a thought the ramifications of which are too numerous to list, none of which I want to consider because I'm hungry and need to get through the turkey meat in my refrigerator, most of which is slimy and likely on the verge of going bad.

I'm at a Seattle club, Havana, and "What Is Love" by Haddaway is playing and the air is suffused with a sense of camaraderie, joy, optimism, and hope. I'm drunkenly dancing which in my case means rhythmically moving my shoulders and I'm lecherously eyeing the attractive women who are in close proximity to me. However I'm somewhat distracted as I'm at the club with my friend, Joel, a man I know from college who's clearly mentally ill. Joel's spent the last decade at a Zen center, the idea for which was planted by me, as while we were in college I talked extensively about what my life was like when I lived at a monastery. I can't say I understand Joel's illness even though I'm well-versed in different diagnoses and their criteria although if I had to say I'm guessing he suffers from bipolar. Joel's been open about his depression and the perpetual struggles he has with anxiety, both of which I've assured him can be addressed with psychiatric medication. "They're not going to make you into a different person," I say. "You'll still be recognizably you." Whenever I've reassured him about this he's invariably said nothing, looking away from me and robotically nodding in response. He'll say, "I don't want to avoid reality," and I'll have to refrain from lashing out, mainly because of the implication he's drawing which is that my use of meds means I'm avoiding some deep existential truth. On the occasions that Joel says this—that he doesn't want to "run away"—I feel the urge to say to him, "Aren't you running away from the world by living at a Zen center?" Instead I bite my tongue and offer him whatever moral support I can, focusing on his life, his problems, everything him him him. The truth is: Joel doesn't care about me and isn't really my friend and he only contacted me on this, his vacation from the Zen center, because he was jockeying for position. He's always felt inferior to me or threatened by me or at the very least deeply competitive with me, as if it were of vital importance to Joel that between the two of us he be the person with a greater degree of wisdom. I'm repulsed by his neediness and narcissism and his desperate need to be victorious but I also have compassion for how broken and sad he must feel. How broken and sad and more than anything how lonely the man must feel to be competitive with someone as broken and sad and lonely as me. In fact it's this mixture of repulsion and compassion that emerges at this very moment at Havana, this moment when Joel starts dancing insanely, like someone out of a Vanilla Ice video. Joel's dancing is sufficiently embarrassing that I don't want to be anywhere near him, a feeling evidently shared by neighboring patrons, all of whom move centrifugally away from Joel. Soon I'm the only person left it's just Joel and me in our corner of the club and it's unclear to me whether Joel's aware of the mass exodus that's occurred. "Joel will hang himself by the time he's fifty," I think to myself as I sadly observe the man's trying-way-too-hard dancing. That's not a moral judgment, mind you. In a sense, I am Joel. Deep down: Joel is me.

Everyone at Zeke's refers to the drunk guy as Butch which is baffling because he doesn't introduce himself that way. Butch is the butt of many jokes and lurches around the living room as he carries a White Claw and Master P booms from the speakers. "Butch, get out of the way!" Zeke yells when the former obstructs the latter's vision of the TV, an obstruction which elicits a series of apologies from Butch. These apologies are pathetic, as if Butch had no dignity at all, and the impression I have is that Butch's function here is to serve as a punching bag to all of the addicts present. He's ridiculed by everyone and has a slavish disposition and often does things like get water for people or take out the garbage. He's a kind of holy fool a drunken and coked out bodhisattva and the central question I have is whether he understands and is accepting of his role. My ultimate conclusion is that he simply wants friends and to be of service, this even though it's not accurate to call anyone at Zeke's his friend. I take pity on the man and try to engage him in conversation which is a challenge that for his part he does his best to meet. However he's easily distractible and the rap music is loud and several conversations are occurring at once on proximate beanbags. I want to optimize his chances for success because in this environment Butch is likely doomed to fail which is to say that in this madhouse his attempts at connection are going to be abortive. "Who's your favorite musician?" I ask him but he's clearly struggling with sensory overload which means that I likely need to perform some sudden act of mercy. I say, "Let's go outside and smoke a cigarette," and Butch seems touched by the offer to spend time together alone and soon we're each outside lighting up our own Camel Crushes. I thank him for the cigarette and ask him if he's a menthol guy or not and Butch's bumbling response makes it clear that this whole endeavor has the potential to be painful. He's a poor conversationalist and clears his throat at semi-regular intervals, both of which irritate me and force me to suppress the impulse to go back inside. I nevertheless proceed and ask him about where he's from, his family, etc., and soon learn that he grew up poor in the Bronx. At eighteen he joined the military and was deployed to Iraq where an IED gave him a TBI and permanently injured his leg. Butch says, "A lot of my Army buddies have killed themselves. The military's no joke. It's as real as it gets." Throughout Butch's narrative I notice a kind of glaze in his eyes which might be the effect of trauma or substance-consumption or both. He then returns to his childhood and discusses how he was extensively bullied at which point the conversation shifts to the perils of expressing vulnerability when you're a man. Butch says, "You can be angry and that's it. Express anything else and people treat you like you're a fucking pussy." I vigorously nod and open my mouth, intending to offer light support but am instead surprised to hear myself confess to being raped as a child. I then talk about how lonely I've always felt and the role that shame plays in that loneliness and just how catastrophic childhood sexual trauma can be to a person's psyche. Butch responds to the moment well, bringing me in for a hug, and though I feel embarrassed by my disclosure I'm reassured by

Butch's warmth. "I love you, man," Butch says after which point he kisses me on the cheek, a gesture it's clear that Butch immediately regrets. I say this because as he pulls away he winces and his eyes refuse to contact mine and he puts out his cigarette as if he's eager to escape my presence. He then says, "Sorry. I'm Greek. We're sometimes a little too much on the affectionate side." I want to reassure the man but realize I have no idea how I would do so as the forces at play in the frail male psyche are much larger than both of us. "It's okay," I say as I put my hand on Butch's shoulder and immediately upon saying this I realize I've uttered a monstrous lie. We're emotionally constricted and the odds are extremely high that we always will be and no banality of mine is going to change that fact at all. Butch then says he'll see me inside and goes back into Zeke's and as I gaze at the sky I again mindlessly repeat, "It's okay. It's going to be okay." We all need lullabies and that's what I'm offering to myself right now I'm singing a lullaby in the hopes that it will help me sleep, if not forever then at least for the night ahead.

"Say what?! I'm partially deaf!" the man, Gunner, yells even though he's seated right next to me on a beanbag chair and the entire spectacle makes me wonder whether I want to repeat my question. "I said do you want to do another line?" a risky question in a room that's this crowded, as everyone's ears have perked up waiting for the answer. Gunner doesn't overtly acknowledge my question but he does gesture with his chin to the door, after which point he pantomimes smoking, a clear invitation to join him outside. I nod my head and soon the two of us are outside and because we're out of the din he has no problems with comprehension. He says, "I heard you hung out with my business partner the other night," and my assumption is that he's got me confused with someone else, as I have no interest in spending time with Zeke-people outside of Zeke's. He says, "Randy. Tall guy. The two us import bamboo. His dad owns the company, and it's mainly run out of Florida." Surprisingly I do know the man in question and in fact have spent time with him outside of Zeke's, as two weeks ago I met this wastrel, Randy, and went to his apartment. I say, "Yeah. Totally. I didn't realize you guys were business partners. Must be pretty tight then, I imagine." The latter comment is duplicitous as Randy spent half of the night talking shit about his then-anonymous business partner but I'm curious to get Gunner's read on the situation. He says, "We used to be, yeah. But business gets in the way, bro. It gets in the way. Like, he sleeps during the days, because he stays up all night doing coke. No judgment on that shit. Not at all. Not my place. But if you're running a business you can't be coked out or asleep every day during business hours." I nod in understanding, pull on my cigarette, and do my best to act engaged but truthfully I'm already impatient to get back inside and see if anyone will offer me a line. I say, "I can see why you're frustrated," at which point I again pull on my cigarette, eager to finish it before I get roped into an elaborate story. Gunner says, "What did Randy say about me? You guys were partying, right?" I say, "He drove me over to his place, yeah. Drove like a lunatic the whole way there. He didn't talk business, really. Mainly wanted to talk about music." Hearing this, Gunner narrows his eyes, as something I've said has clearly piqued his interest. I learn what it is when he opens his mouth again. He says, "Drove like a lunatic, huh? I'll show you what it means to drive like a lunatic. I actually race cars. Randy probably didn't tell you that, did he?" I shake my head slowly, clearly detached from the conversation, and I'm ready to stub out my cigarette early when Gunner finds the way to ensnare me. He says, "I heard you inside, by the way. I know you want to do more coke. If you come to my car, we can do some, and then I can drive us around." Gunner now has my attention and although I'm scared to go driving with some coked-out speed demon I agree to follow the man to his car. Before we do so I say, "You want to do some first? A couple key bumps right here?" and Gunner vigorously shakes his head in answer to the questions. He says, "Not out here, bro. Not in public. We'll do some when we get to my ride. And then we'll find somewhere the two of us can fly." I nod but I'm frustrated and only reluctantly do I follow after Gunner and two blocks later we arrive at what looks like a red Corvette. We each get in the car and I immediately ask to do a bump, at which point Gunner says, "Take it easy, bro. Give me time to get out my bag." Gunner then reaches into a pocket and pulls out what looks like 1.5 grams and after he takes two key bumps I do the same. The bumps minimally affect me as I've done a gram every day for the past two weeks and at this point I'm mainly using the drug to maintain some sort of psychic equilibrium. What does affect me however is the prospect of going 120 down some backroad in Lynnwood, the thought of which makes me feel panicked. I say, "I have to tell you something, Gunner," not knowing exactly what I'm going to say, only that I need to dissemble somehow so that I can extricate myself from the situation. I say, "I dig your energy. I do. But my cousin died while he was speed-racing. So while I'm down to hang with you, I don't want to go driving." Gunner purses his lips and nods and seems unsurprised by what I've said, at which point he says, "What kind of car was your cousin driving?" I say, "I don't know. Not an expensive one," to which Gunner says, "Probably made in America," after which he mindlessly stares out through his windshield. He then says, "That's too bad about your cousin. And it's too bad we can't go for a ride. Just so you know though: you should really work out your shit." I then step out of the vehicle and am braced by the cold air and the sight of the moon and also by the knowledge that I've been seen so clearly, that a lie can so beautifully give rise to the truth.

It's 7 AM and I'm preparing to go running when I receive an onslaught of audio messages from Bill. Among other things he says, "I'm fine," "Don't worry," "It doesn't matter," etc., although these phrases are disconnected and bookmarked by gibberish. He's obviously drunk and is likely doing cocaine and because I have to go to work soon I'm reluctant to get roped into a conversation. Nevertheless I do get roped in and soon I'm sending him audio messages myself, messages that talk about me minimally but mainly express concern for him. Bill slurs in his responses and seems unable to remain fixed on any one train of thought and this scatteredness makes it impossible to have anything resembling an actual conversation. I say, "We'll talk when you're sober. Go to bed. There's no use in trying to have a convo right now," and Bill seems to comply with this because I don't receive any more audio messages. Then on the drive to work I imagine what it will be like in the future when I get the phone call that Bill has overdosed or committed suicide or etc. I put on the Chili Peppers' "By the Way," a vintage karaoke song for Bill, and as the chorus hits I tear up remembering all the times I did karaoke with him. There was always a purity to his performances, a purity born of a lack of concern for his audience, a lack of concern I envied given how consumed I always was with how my own performances were received. Bill often said that I'd made him more attuned to the importance of audience, as contrastingly I've often said Bill has taught me to be more vocal about who I am and what I believe. But so as I drive down the highway, as I think back on what Bill has meant to me, it occurs to me that I'm already thinking of our relationship in a retrospective fashion. Like it's dead. Like Bill is dead. Like what we had together has already died. Which isn't all that strange if you think about it actually. Because there's no going back. It's gone. All of it. Every last little bit. Everything I've known and loved in my life is in some basic sense already dead.

I'm in Lafayette, Louisiana, and I've been at my social work job for almost a month, a job that involves me making house calls to all manner of poverty-stricken psychotics. Abbeville, Carencro, New Iberia, etc.; parts of these cities contain the worst poverty I've ever seen. Weather-beaten street signs, houses of ancient decaying wood; to me, an outsider, these cities seem blasted, vaguely post-apocalyptic. However on this particular morning I've been asked to meet with a woman on the outskirts of Lafayette and when I arrive I'm greeted with a big ornate house that may or may not qualify as a mansion. As I walk up to the stately door I recall my experience at work yesterday which among other things involved entering a cockroach-infested trailer in New Iberia. There were of course tree roaches in the trailer but the infestation was mainly comprised of the smaller, less repulsive roaches, the latter of which could be glimpsed everywhere one chose to rest one's eyes. On the ground, on the walls, on the fabric of the couch, etc. The trailer felt alive, like it itself skittered about and was capable of respiration. A mother and daughter lived in the trailer and the matriarch, Dolores, was morbidly obese, to such an extreme degree that she didn't seem able to leave her bed. However it serves to reason that she did because her daughter, Brandi, would invariably have complained if she had had to escort her mother to the restroom. The visit to the trailer, my first, had been utterly surreal, as the sheer quantity of cockroaches was so large as to almost bypass my disgust. "Have you been experiencing any depression?" I recall asking first Dolores and then Brandi, a nest of cockroaches blooming like a flower on Dolores's headboard after I did so. Shockingly at least to me neither woman reported any depressive symptoms, living proof that a person can become habituated to and even thrive in virtually any environment. I felt proud of myself when I left, like I was a gladiator who'd survived a fight at the Coliseum, but the moment I entered my car I began to experience phantom sensations. Namely I was convinced that cockroaches were crawling on my clothes and it took me several minutes to calm down enough for these sensations to abate. Contrast this to the present experience, wherein a slender woman answers the door to the mansion, and after I tentatively introduce myself—"I'm with an organization called NHS.

I think I have an appointment to see someone here named Elizabeth?"—I'm ushered past the foyer into a palatial kitchen. The woman sits down at the kitchen table and invites me to do the same and then introduces herself as Beth. I proceed to provide Beth with my opening spiel which involves a discussion of HIPAA, services offered, etc., at which point I ask Beth if she'd be willing to tell me about herself. She says, "To start off with, I don't live here. This is my brother's house, and he works in oil. That's why it's so nice and big, as I'm sure you've come to notice." I say, "Have you always lived with your brother?" after which Beth looks away ashamedly and whispers, "Only for a month. Six weeks at the absolute most." I attempt to project understanding but the truth is I don't yet understand and so I sit in silence with Beth waiting for her to continue. She says, "My house in Broussard burned down. I didn't have anywhere else to go. My brother's a kindly man, so he's letting me stay here until I get on my feet." I say, "I'm sorry about your house. That must have been quite the traumatic event," to which she says, "Maybe. But I did set the fire myself." I'm uncertain as to the woman's motives so I wait for her to say more which means that when she doesn't I'm forced to inquire directly. She then says, "I was inside the house when I set the fire. I was trying to burn myself alive. My husband had just left me, and I saw no reason to go on living." I say, "Are you still struggling with suicidal feelings?" to which she says, "Yeah. Definitely. Of course. Nothing's changed for me, and I still don't see the point." I conduct an inventory of myself and am amazed that I'm not especially triggered by the woman's words, which means I think that I've made progress in processing the death of

Bob. I then conduct a standard interview with Beth, asking her further questions about her psychiatric history, her use of psych meds, her coping mechanisms, etc. At meeting's end as I'm leaving she says, "I like the energy I get from you, young man. I think we'll work well together. Even if I will probably always want to die." I then shake the woman's hand, say goodbye, and walk out to my car, at which point I mutter, "Good things are happening all the time." I then smile and feel content and open the driver's side door, at which point I'm greeted with the sight of a large tree roach skittering across my seat.

I'm twelve years old and I'm horny and I'm masturbating in my bathroom in Puyallup, specifically to the imagined sight of me being fellated by a girl in school named Sierra. I've already masturbated five times today five or six who's really counting and as I do so yet again I begin to approach another orgasm. However as I come upon the threshold one of my dogs, Chelsea, starts to bark though what exactly at I haven't the foggiest, as she's a dog whose wont is to spontaneously begin barking. In any case when she barks I instantaneously hatch a grisly plan, the execution of which plan I know I'll later find to be grotesque. But of course now isn't later so I proceed headlong into the hideous plan which involves first exiting the bathroom and then retrieving a jar of Jif from a kitchen cupboard. I then bring the Jif jar to the bathroom and after locking the door I put a globule of peanut butter on my corona and then crouch down in front of my dachshunds, Chelsea and Sascha, and allow them to lick the peanut butter off my penis. I shift away from the dogs when I start to cum but sickeningly they follow after me and lick my ejaculate, a development that causes me to feel a profound degree of disgust. I try to comfort myself by saying, "Some of my friends have probably done this, too," not having any firm idea of whether or not that's true, nor would I want to know if it is because the behavior is so revolting. "If that's true, is that a good thing?" and I don't know the question's answer, because while being defective is painful, it may not be as painful as knowing that everyone is defective, that everyone is damaged, that everyone has secrets they'd rather die with than share with anyone else on earth.

I haven't called my mother in a week which is a tactical error on my part because my successful exploitation of her hinges on regular contact. If we go too long without conversing my mother thinks that something is wrong which realistically there is because it means I've been staying up all night doing drugs. I decide to call my mother in the next ten minutes but not before I do at least two lines which is the bare minimum I think for me to feel alert and engaged in our conversation. I open my cupboard and retrieve my baggie and razor and right before I dump out the cocaine I mutter, "You don't need two lines just to talk to your mother." Nevertheless despite my pep talk I still dump out over a tenth of a gram and begin to mindlessly cut it up with my razor. Tellingly however I cut the large quantity into a single line, a line I proceed to do in one fell swoop of my nostril. I cough and shimmy my head and then wait a minute before I call my mother and when she answers I feel like fear is unknown to me and that I'm ready to bare my soul.

The story I've written about my father, Charles, is appropriately enough entitled "Charles," and it's less a story than thinly veiled autobiography. It's the first real story I've ever completed and in my way I'm proud of what I've written although invariably it's flawed as any story about my father would be. That is to say that while the story might be complete it's decidedly incomplete as it's impossible to capture the true complexity of my father. Still nevertheless I make the decision to share my story, "Charles," with Charles and after he reads it he responds with his predictable mixture of rage and indignation. He calls me an ingrate and says I'm pathetic for not having successfully moved past my childhood—"Get over it!"— and makes himself into a victim for having such an ingrate of a son. My mother meanwhile who's codependent calls me out for writing the story, calling it cruel and vicious and tantamount to character assassination. That in fact is the phrase they both return to—"What you've written is character assassination, Michael"—and when I ask them to point out where I've lied or embellished upon the truth they are unable to do so. Soon after reading the story my father removes me from his will and tells me over the phone that he's disgusted to call himself my father. The whole ordeal is baffling and emotionally taxing because when I examine my motives for writing the story what predominates isn't the desire to inflict pain on my father. I simply wanted to depict the man clearly. To reckon with who he is and who he's been. However to do so was evidently verboten by my parents. "I was just trying to be honest," I tell my father. "As a writer, you must know what that's like." To which he responds, "You're nothing like me, boy. You couldn't be honest if you tried." I say nothing in response and the man hands the phone back to my mother, after which she says, "So did you two work it out?"

The first Gulf War has begun and I'm writing a letter to a soldier, an action I've embarked upon at the request of my second-grade teacher. I talk about myself including my desire to play in the NBA but what's much more important to me is that I learn about my addressee. Where are they from? What are their hobbies? What is it like in Iraq and do they like the people there? I ask these and related questions in the hopes that I can gain a pen pal in the service. All of which is to say: the experience of writing the letter is absolutely unremarkable or at least it is until I arrive at the ultimate sentence of the page-long letter. That sentence in its entirety is: "Saddam Hussein must not be underestimated." In the years that follow I'll identify this moment as the foundational moment of my literary life, specifically my use of the word "underestimated," a word that at this time I don't fully comprehend. In fact it's precisely this pseudo-comprehension, this nascent awareness of the word's strangely allusive and elusive power, that makes me feel like the moment marks the dawning of a new era. Language has become beautiful and imperfect and capable of both denoting objects and connoting ideas, none of which of course I can articulate right now as a second-grader. Right now all I know is that the word strikes me as almost magical in its power, as if the word, "underestimate," both is a word and is entirely not. And although it sounds strange to say it the moment thus also represents the beginning of my religious sensibility, at least insofar as it heightens my awareness of a different world, a world comprised solely of words. "Finish up," Mrs. Biven says, and though I have more to say I just sign my name at the end of the letter. Because there's no topping the final sentence. So why even try?

While he's obviously damaged, Jim, my workshop mate, is a talented writer who is also extraordinarily smart. He writes autobiographical fiction, all of which takes place during the Iraq war, and when I read his stories I feel a twinge of envy. The man baffles me to be honest, as he's thoughtful and interesting yet also inexplicably chose to enlist in the Marines. One day we're in his room smoking pot—Jim hates my writing but enjoys my company— when I decide to violate decorum and ask him about his service. I say, "Did you ever kill anybody, Jim?" He shrugs his shoulders and looks away and then after taking a hit from the bowl he says, "I threw a grenade into a room and blew a guy to bits." I nod slowly, waiting for more, but Jim is content to say nothing which means that I'm going to have to take the conversational reins. "Do you think you have PTSD?" I ask, knowing the answer to be yes, but I'm intrigued to see how he views his situation. He says, "I have nightmares, sure. So in a way. Yeah, I guess. And if I don't have weed it's basically impossible for me to relax." I say, "What's the treatment for that? Do you take psych meds for sleep?" Jim scoffs at the question and then puts some chaw into his mouth. He says, "That shit don't work. And it makes you fat as a hog. I don't have no interest in supporting pharmaceutical companies, so I'll stick to weed, thank you very much." I take a hit from the bowl and nod and as I blow out a plume of smoke I ask him if he's heard of the studies where MDMA is used as a novel treatment for trauma. He says, "I heard about that, yeah. I call bullshit on that, too. Ain't no drug going to get the sight of dead bodies out of your mind." As I regard the man before me I say to myself, "You don't really know Jim at all," and because of this I feel the need to cut to the core of the issue. I say, "Jim, you're a thoughtful and sensitive guy. Why in the world did you choose to enlist?" after which he spits chaw juice into a Styrofoam cup. He says, "Because I wanted to kill some motherfuckers. That's the long and the short of it really. I wanted to kill a motherfucking human being." I assume I look aghast because Jim says, "Don't look so shocked. We're not so different, you and me," after which he pauses and says, "But maybe I'm wrong. Maybe you're just a pussy who wants to spend every day thinking about art." Surprisingly I'm not offended though I'm uncertain of how to respond to the comment but in the end I hand the bowl back to Jim and say, "I do like to think about art."

Two kids in my math class at Ferrucci junior high approach me and ask me to help them get stoned. I'm uniquely suited or so it seems to serve as an intermediary between the wastrels and the intellectually "gifted" students because I've been grouped into the latter class while still associating with the former. The two students, Wes and Brandon, have no interest in purchasing a bag or buying a pipe but are instead simply looking to experience the effects of marijuana. They offer to pay me $40 for my assistance, an offer I happily accept, and the three of us arrange to meet on the school grounds at 10 PM on the following Saturday night. While all of us recognize that this is a dubious choice for location we agree to it because of the school's proximity to Wes' house. The early stages of the plan go off without a hitch and soon Wes and Brandon are each taking hits off of my Cobra-shaped bong. I encourage them to each take at least seven or eight hits because in my experience it's difficult to get high the first time you smoke pot. Eight large hits seem like a sufficiently large quantity however that a threshold would be crossed and intoxication would be guaranteed for Wes and Brandon. By the end of the smoking session it's clear that both boys are experiencing the effects of the drug, as evidenced by their constant giggling and their seeming unsteadiness on their feet. I'm due to return to the house of my friend, Abe—which is where I told my parents I was spending the night—but before leaving the two boys I seek reassurance from them that they're in positive casts of mind. "We feel great," Brandon says, to which Wes adds, "I feel fucking awesome, Keen. You're the best," and after hearing this I feel greatly reassured. The following morning I call Wes in order to inquire into how the rest of the boys' night unfolded and am greeted by the sound of Wes' mother's voice. She asks to speak to my mother which obviously immediately unnerves me but I comply with the request and soon learn what's occurred. Apparently after we parted ways Brandon and Wes broke into the school and wandered the hallways not knowing motion detectors were present. Policemen then came and ended up arresting the two boys, at which point they were transferred to Remann Hall, a juvenile detention facility. Brandon and Wes' parents then come over to my house and talk to my mom and dad about the dangers we all face as young drug users. In the midst of doing so Brandon's father turns to me and says, "If you ever contact my son again I'll be on you like flies on shit." The day after this I go to school and am expelled from ninth grade, this even though Brandon and Wes—who were the ones who broke into the school—are only suspended for five days. When high school begins Wes will be nowhere to be found which I learn from a mutual friend is because he was sent to a military academy. Brandon for his part will become a heavy marijuana smoker and will from what I gather regularly consume psychedelics. This is all hearsay however as ironically enough I stay away from Brandon because I'm attempting to abstain from drugs and to commit my energies to high school debate. A decade later in a fit of curiosity and nostalgia I search for Wes and Brandon on Myspace. Wes I can't find but Brandon I locate and based on his profile it's clear he's in early recovery from an addiction to crystal meth. Though it shouldn't, this flabbergasts me and precipitates an upwelling of remorse, namely because I was the person who introduced Brandon to drugs. I decide to message Brandon and to make minimal small-talk, as realistically I have no interest in nourishing a relationship with the man. Instead I apologize straightaway, asking for the man's forgiveness, and tell him I wish I had never gotten him stoned all that time ago. He says, "Thanks for the message. But you're not responsible for my decisions. I made my bed, so I have to lie in it, you know?" I tell him I do and then log off and then afterward I'm overcome with the feeling of gratitude but not because I've been absolved of any wrongdoing. No. I'm grateful because Brandon was the fuckup and Brandon's the one who became an addict which means I'm better than him and that existentially I've won. Or so I tell myself at the time when I'm still foolish enough to think that life is a competition which actually from a certain vantage it is if you can acknowledge that it's a competition that one day we're each going to lose.

William is heavily lesioned and dying of AIDS and his only request when I enter the bedroom is that he be moved to the living room couch. He doesn't have a wheelchair or a walker or a cane or etc., nor does he have the strength or energy to lift himself out of bed. This means that if I'm going to honor William's request I'm going to have to improvise somehow, an improvisation I'm certain I'm not capable of performing. Luckily the hospice chaplain is present and he seems relatively intelligent or at least he strikes me as more intelligent than I am in the context of mechanical problem-solving. I say, "How do we get him into the living room?" to which the chaplain shrugs his shoulders, imperturbable to a degree that I find to be strange. It occurs to me then that the chaplain is a dullard like me, utterly incapable of devising a novel mechanical solution. He says, "How about I grab his arms and you grab his legs? It's not far. We'll just drag him over to the couch." The plan strikes me as grotesque and inhumane but I see no better way of moving William and after asking William if he consents to this he offers the subtlest of nods. The chaplain, Morris, and I then proceed to execute the plan, and as we move I'm astonished by the lightness of William. "God, he's so fucking light!" I say to Morris when we're out of earshot of William, after which I remember that Morris is a man of the cloth. I say, "My apologies for the profanity," after which Morris impassively shakes his head. He then says, "I may be a believer, brother, but that doesn't mean my shit doesn't fucking stink."

I'm with Abe and Danny and we're seeking cover behind a copse of trees as we smoke pot in a bespoke pipe made from a soda can. We smoke two bowls between the three of us and toss the can when we're finished and then walk out from the copse onto a basketball court attached to Wildwood park. Abe asks me if I'm stoned and I'm prepared to say no which means that I've now smoked pot twice without it having any discernible effect. However when I say the word, "No," I realize that my mind is in fact altered, as evidenced by the extraordinary strangeness of my voice. I say, "Does my voice sound strange to you?" after which Abe and Danny erupt in laughter, and soon thereafter I too am in hysterics. Danny says, "It's not even funny!" as the three of us lurch across a basketball court, and it's at this stage that I fully comprehend what it means to be stoned. "It's like a photo," I say, referring to the present experience, an experience that seems to exist outside of the realm of temporal continuity. "Snapshots," I say. "It's just one snapshot after another," and after saying this Abe says, "Keen, you're fucked up as hell!" And yes while what he says is true it's also true that this moment is providing me with genuine insight, at least insofar as it's teaching me how disconnected the present is from every moment that's come before. "Every moment we begin again," I mutter and neither Danny or Abe hear what I've said, which is for the best I think as people want to believe who they are is who they've always been. I then stare up at the evening sky and observe the countless pinpricks of light and feel gratitude for this moment, the only moment that's real. I then say, "Where do we go from here?" and I'm not exactly sure what I mean, but Danny hears me and answers without missing a beat. He sings, "We went down, down, down. And the flames went higher," after which point Abe and I join in and sing, "And it burns, burns, burns. The ring of fire. The ring of fire. The ring of fire. The ring of fire."

My mom is reminiscing about my German babysitter, Oma Leini, when she says, "It's just awful what happened to her brother." I have no idea what she's referencing so I ask my mother to clarify and when I do she says, "You know. What happened with the Nazis." Again I tell my mother that I have no clue what she's referring to, at which point she scoffs exasperatedly on the phone. She says, "I've told you this story before. About how the Nazis came to Oma Leini's house. About how her brother refused to join the Nazis so they shot him in the head in front of the family in the living room." The information floors me and I envision my babysitter rushing to a boy while his head hemorrhages blood, a gruesome image that I shake my head to try to escape. I say, "Jesus Christ, Mom. How have you never told me this story?" at which point my mother, still exasperated, insists that she has. I say, "I think I'd remember this story if you had told me. It's not something I'd just forget." My mom says, "I don't know what's wrong with you. I told you and your sister. I can even remember the moment I told you." I call bullshit on this as well and tell my mom I'll call her back in five minutes, at which point I call my sister and tell her the story. I say, "Do you remember ever hearing that story?" and Annie is clearly equally flabbergasted, at which point I immediately call back my mother. I say, "Annie doesn't remember it either, Mom. Which means you never told us the story." My mom then says, "Oh, well. Probably for the best. No need to let children know the truth. They figure it out anyway in the long run, no matter how bad it is."

My coworker, Isabella, tells me that she's separating from her husband and after she does so I immediately feel the stirrings of an erection. "I'm sorry to hear that," I say. "Do you want to get a drink and talk about it after work?" We agree to meet at 7 at The Canterbury on Capitol Hill and when we meet up Isabella's wearing a black strapless dress. I buy her a vodka soda and myself a whiskey ginger and soon we're each jabbering about our jobs, our romantic histories, etc. After three drinks each we leave Canterbury and go to my apartment where we first have sex and then engage in post-coital chit-chat. I then walk with Isabella to her car where we proceed to again have sex and when we part ways I rue the decisions I've made. I think to myself, "Hopefully this wasn't a fuck-up," and then I shrug my shoulders and walk back to my place, recognizing that there's nothing to be done. As I lie down to go to sleep I ask myself if sleeping with Isabella was predatory, a legitimate question given that she's just separated from her husband of thirteen years. However the answer's fairly clearly unclear as for instance Isabella is fifteen years older than I am and at forty-four she should be capable of making her own decisions. Plus it's not my responsibility to decide whether a decision is wise for another person, as the only thing I can control is my own personal behavior. Or at least this is what I tell myself as I replay the intercourse that's just occurred which is what occupies my mind until I drift off to sleep. The following day at work Isabella comes into my office and begins to aggressively rub my penis above my pants. I improvise a lie about how I don't want to get seriously involved because I'm hung up on my ex-girlfriend, Zoe, and am trying to reconcile with her. Of course Isabella doesn't care and looks at me lasciviously and she soon takes my hand and guides it up her skirt. Soon we're fucking in my work's restroom and I'm as turned on as I've ever been which is baffling to me given how Isabella looks. All of which is to say: Isabella isn't attractive and one reason I'm so turned on is that I'm disgusted by my attraction. In her presence I feel embodied, embodied and thus consequently real and that's because I find her to be borderline physically grotesque. Her ugliness in other words makes me acutely aware of the primacy of the body and in doing so makes me acutely aware of my own animal nature. These at least are the thoughts that flutter about my mind as I take my place back at my desk after the restroom episode has occurred. Soon thereafter I learn I've been accepted to Syracuse's MFA program which among other reasons I'm grateful for because it provides me with an exit strategy from Isabella. Yes the sex we have is glorious and yes it's utterly dehumanizing but in its way it's the most rooted in my body I've been in my entire life. I'm confused in other words as I don't even want to be seen in public with Isabella, though in private I'm so turned on by her that it feels impossible to quaff my sexual thirst. On my final day at work Isabella says, "I just don't get it. We fuck so, so, so, so well. Why don't you want to be with me, Michael?" and instantly I think of my experience with Deborah. Honesty doesn't always serve us and in this situation it should absolutely be avoided, as it would be supremely hurtful to tell Isabella, "I'm disgusted by you and how ugly you are." Nevertheless I have to provide a reason so I repeat the oft-practiced lie which is to say that I'm still emotionally monogamous with Zoe. Isabella sighs and says, "Your loss," at which point she lifts up her skirt and gestures at the restroom. She says, "One more for old times' sake?" and I stand up with an erection blooming in my pants. I just can't seem to reconcile who I am with who I see myself to be.

Zeke's silent in his recliner as he watches *The Goonies* and as he does so I entertain the notion that he's dead. On countless occasions I've had similar thoughts about myself, specifically the thought that I'm presently in some purgatorial wasteland. Based on what I've read paranoia of this nature is common, an extreme version of which is called the Cotard delusion. As I sit here coked out and vaguely attending to the film I wonder whether I meet the threshold for an actual diagnosis of Cotard. I then idly mutter, "It wouldn't be a delusion if I'm actually dead," and the whispered utterance prompts Zeke to ask me to repeat myself. "Oh, nothing," I say, eager to change the subject entirely, in part because I'm amped up and need to somehow channel my excess energy. I ask, "How are you doing, Zeke?" which Zeke responds to with a shrug of the shoulders, after which point he says, "I'm fine, bro. You know: can't complain." I lean forward in my beanbag chair and then say, "Yeah, yeah, yeah. But how are you *really* doing, Zeke?" and when Zeke looks at me I can see he's considering several questions. Can I actually be trusted? Is my desire to connect purely the result of me doing coke? And if Zeke confides in me how honest should he choose to be? Zeke then says, "My pops died a month ago. Not a tragedy or nothin. He lived a full life, and you can't ask for a whole lot more than that." I vigorously nod, manically grateful to have been granted entry into Zeke's inner circle, or at least what in my drugged-out state I tell myself is Zeke's inner circle. I say, "Wow. That's heavy. Are you doing okay with it, Zeke? And what was your relationship like with your dad?" "Frosty," Zeke says. "We had our ups and our downs. But I got to say goodbye to him. So we had our moment, you know what I mean?" I mindlessly nod as I mull over which path I should take by which I mean should I wait for Zeke to offer more details or should I attempt to solicit them? I err toward the former by saying, "I'm glad you got some closure. Not everyone gets that, Zeke." Zeke eyes me warily, either warily or kindly—I can't tell—and eventually he says, "You're not like the other folks that come here. You know that, right?" The moment gives me pause, in part because of the rebuke implicit in the comment—does he think I'm too good for a trap house?—but also because of his concern for me, a concern that's at odds with his concern with the bottom line. I say, "I appreciate your concern. It means a lot to me, man. But I feel at home here. I don't want to leave anytime soon." Zeke grimaces and grabs the remote, evidently eager to drown me out by turning up the volume on *The Goonies*. As he does so he says, "I ain't concerned. It's like they say: you are the company you keep. You may not belong here now, Mike, but shit, maybe one day you will."

At Victoria's insistence she texts me a link to her FetLife account, one that has countless photos of her being essentially tortured. There are photos of her being whipped, wearing a leash, gagging on penises, etc., but what's most perturbing are the photos of her being tied up and contorted into painful positions. Her body seems to float above the ground because of the array of ligature that's been used, ligature that includes rope but also metal bindings and etc. In fact the photos look vaguely medieval, like Victoria's been drawn and is poised to be quartered, and as I gaze at them Victoria asks me what I think. I say, "What do you mean exactly? Like, am I turned on as a result of seeing the photos? Because if that's what you're asking, the answer is no." Victoria bites her lip nervously but otherwise doesn't react to what I've said which makes my wheels spin about how to proceed. Should I end the relationship immediately? Would it be cruel to do so right after she's shown me her account? I don't know but it's clear our relationship is doomed. I suspected this earlier when Victoria confessed to having engaged in knife play in the past, the description of which practice made me profoundly uneasy. Victoria then says, "Do you still want to try to be together?" which means she's giving me a clear exit strategy, one that I'd likely avail myself of if I were honorable and brave. Sadly I'm not really honorable nor am I particularly brave which means that I postpone addressing the issue by saying, "We can still try to make it work." However in the weeks that follow I become increasingly paranoid, specifically in terms of my concern that Victoria is sexually unsatisfied on some elemental level. She says, "I'm happy with our sex life. Bondage is only one part of who I am," a line that sounds canned and that I mostly disbelieve. I then say, "But it's a big part, right? Masochism is at the core of your sexual identity. Which makes us incompatible, because I'm not much of a sadist." As before we discuss the issue and as before we get nowhere, partly because of my inertia and partly because of Victoria's denial. I know it's going to end and on some level so does she and in fact it does end two and a half weeks later. The breakup occurs when Victoria and I go to Alki beach and sit on some boulders and stare at the wild hues that emerge during sunset. She says, "I think we're better off as friends," a comment with which I agree but don't respond, and because of my silence Victoria feels compelled to continue. She says, "I don't think you're a provider," which I view as comic in an abstract, cerebral sort of way, which is to say I don't actually laugh at the comment though I do wait for her to continue. She says, "I need a provider. It might not sound feminist or whatever. But I need a man to provide for me. That's what I'm looking for, I think." I consider how to respond—do I focus on the absurdity of a progressive woman ceding to 1950s gender stereotypes?—when it occurs to me: we don't choose how we feel. Yes Victoria's thoughts are probably socially regressive but do I really care about that on any level whatsoever? She's being honest about her experience which is more than I've been doing with mine and consequently I have to tip my hat at the woman. "I understand," I say. "Breaking up is probably a good idea." She then says, "Are you mad at me, Michael? And do you understand what I mean?" I nod and look at the waves, the sounds of which are comforting at present, and when I speak again I too try to be honest. I say, "I get it. You think I'm weak. Weak and feminine. Or at least not masculine. And it all boils down to sex: you don't want to fuck a man who isn't masculine." I'm surprised by my intensity and candor and fully expect Victoria to say something conciliatory when she says, "Yeah. That about it covers it, I think."

Dan's an alcoholic asshole who constantly interrupts others when they speak and yet despite my loathing for him I'm in his apartment. At present Dan's interrupting Grayson, a philosophy professor who struck it rich investing in the stock market, and he's starting to lecture Grayson on the definition of anti-natalism. Grayson patiently waits for Dan's tirade to end and when it does he says, "I published a journal article on the topic. So I think I'm pretty well-versed in anti-natalism, Dan." Dan continues to bloviate which utterly disgusts me and so in an attempt to tune him out I cut out lines for me, Grayson, and Bill. Dan says, "You're not going to cut a line for me?" which prompts me to roll my eyes and say, "Dan, you've never asked for a line of coke. Not once. Not ever. And I've done cocaine here a lot." Incidentally it will only be in a year, after I've relapsed after an extended period of sobriety, that I'll actually come to understand what it means to do cocaine a lot. Dan in any case seems bored by me cutting up the coke and so he walks out onto his balcony to smoke a cigarette with Bill. After he does so it's just me and Grayson on the couch and because I'm coked out I want to profoundly connect with the man. We've done drugs together before but the topics—music, film, etc.—were rather anodyne on those occasions and tonight I'd like to solidify our bond. Happily enough the opportunity to do so presented itself earlier when Grayson removed a sweater he was wearing and exposed scar tissue on his wrists. I say, "This might be too much to talk about. But we're both lit up, Grayson, so I think you'll be game. Is it okay if I talk to you about something personal?" Grayson shrugs his shoulders and yawns and seems extremely at peace in the present moment which given the amount of coke we've done I find to be bizarre. He says, "Sure, dude. Fire away," and I assess his entire person for signs he's on cocaine, the only indicators being mild jaw movement and a slight shaking of his hands. I say, "I see the scarring on your wrists. Is that the result of a suicide attempt?" after which question he again shrugs his shoulders and yawns. He says, "I tried to kill myself in Paris. Was in the hospital for several days. Only survived by the skin of my teeth." I vigorously nod, as if I am a tourist being supplied with directions, and then ask him what the circumstances were. He says, "Oh, you know. Typical adolescent-type shit. I was twenty and had been reading Rimbaud . . . There are different ways to interpret it, I guess. A psychiatrist would say I suffered from major depression, and that the depression simply didn't manifest itself until I reached the age of twenty. My mom and dad, in contrast, would say that at that time I hadn't yet found what I was passionate about, and that that lack of passion made me not want to live." Grayson pauses his narrative at this point because I offer him a rolled-up dollar bill, at which point he snorts his line and I soon thereafter snort mine. He continues, "As for me? I'd say I just saw the matter very clearly. Life is meaningless, and there's no point in sticking around." Puzzled, I say, "So why *are* you sticking around?" Immediately after I say this I put my hand on the man's shoulder, as I realize the inappropriateness of my comment. I say, "I'm obviously not recommending—" at which point Grayson holds out his hand in a gesture for me to stop, and then says, "It's quite all right. It's a legitimate question." He then points at my baggie on the table, non-verbally asking if we can do another line, and I nod and begin to cut up a tiny rock. He continues, "This is where my anti-natalism comes in. I think it's unethical to bring life into existence. But, once you're here, it's possible for life to be worth it on balance. That's the long and the short of it. No need to get bogged down in minutiae. Once you're here, there are creature comforts to be had." I say, "Such as?" which causes Grayson to laugh, at which point he says, "Cocaine, for one. Good wine. Good sex. Good art. Even something simple, like finding a nice place to watch a sunset." I largely agree with Grayson and so see no reason to scrutinize whether life is actually worth it but nevertheless I'm still curious about the circumstances of the suicide attempt. I say, "You survived by the skin of your teeth. What do you mean by that exactly?" He says, "I was unconscious in a hotel room. Five more minutes and I would have died. The only reason I didn't is that my body was discovered by a maid. If she hadn't come in to change the sheets I'd be dead. I think about that a lot, actually. About the multiverse. In most other universes, I'm dead." Bill then comes in from the balcony and asks us what we've been discussing before saying, "I actually don't care. I just want to do a line." I've yet to finish cutting up the rock so Grayson hands Bill the dollar bill, at which point Bill does the line that's still on the table. He coughs and then says, "So what were you all talking about?" I look to Grayson for guidance on how to answer the question, at which point he matter-of-factly says, "My suicide attempt." Bill looks disgusted and shakes his head and then says, "Sorry to be the asshole. But I'm going to shut that shit down. I want to have a good time tonight, not talk about shit like that." Grayson shrugs his shoulders and says, "That's fine by me," but I feel offended on his behalf. Consequently I say, "Fuck that, Bill. If Grayson needs to process something, we should be available for him to process it." Suddenly Grayson looks upset and begins to shake his head, at which point he looks at me and says, "Listen asshole, you asked *me*. I don't need to process shit. I love life. It's a beautiful thing." I'm taken aback by the hostility and when I glance at Bill I can see that he is too. Grayson then laughs and says, "I'm fucking with you, dude. Life is worthless. It probably would have been better if I died. It's all trash. All of it. Every jot and tittle."

Electrodes are on my skull because I'm getting an EEG, the reason for which is that I'm convinced that I'm brain-damaged. I convinced my parents to get me the EEG in the aftermath of my experience with Hawaiian baby woodrose seeds—a psychedelic—during which in the last two months I've felt intellectually compromised. I can't focus and I'm moody and I feel like my mnemonic recall is impaired, the sum total of which symptoms leave me convinced I've done permanent damage. The Filipino nurse who's applying the electrodes asks me why I'm getting an EEG and when I tell her—"I want to see if my drug use has caused brain damage"—she shakes her head and laughs. She says, "Son, I smoked marijuana every day for thirty years. If anyone should be brain-dead, it's me. You're going to be fine. We both are. There's nothing to fear. God is all about love and forgiveness." I ruminate on the ultimate sentence as my brain waves are measured by the EEG and when I return home an hour later my sister asks me what I learned. I say, "I learned that my brain works just fine. At least according to the EEG," but deep down what I really want to say is, "Today I learned that God is a God of love and forgiveness."

It's Christmas morning in the year 2000 and I'm at home with my family and my mom, my sister, and I are opening presents while my dad watches television. He's drinking Jim Beam and has the eyes of a shark and eventually my mother cajoles him to join us. He seems bored and frustrated and asks why there aren't more presents for him, this though he didn't purchase a present for anyone, as my mother does all the Christmas shopping. At this moment I hate my father and want to gouge out his eyes or at least do something that causes the man pain. I turn to my mother and say, "Dad bought me the psychedelic that fucked up my brain a year ago. He used his credit card to buy the seeds off of the internet." Now my mother's jaw is agape and she stares at my father in disbelief and seconds later she begins keening. "What have you done?!" my mother screams at my father over and over again and for his part he shrugs his shoulders and says, "Michael didn't take them in the way that you're supposed to." Soon my mother leaves the room and my sister does too and the only people left in the living room are me and my father. He says, "You're a little shit, you know that?" and I again see the shark-like look in his eyes and my only regret is that I didn't do enough to make the motherfucker bleed.

Harborview's emergency room is expectedly grim and when I arrive I say to myself, "A hospital is a modern-day charnel house." The seats behind the nursing station are filled with all manner of the destitute and broken and as I wheel Oscar, a client, to triage I feel like I'm being contaminated. "What exactly is the problem?" says a young buxom beautiful nurse, at which point I force myself to not attend to the woman's beauty. I say, "I work at a homeless shelter in Bellevue. Oscar was transported to us from Swedish Hospital in Edmonds. Unfortunately, Oscar's too medically compromised to stay at the shelter. We're just not equipped to deal with him. I know that the social workers here are good with placement. I'm sorry to kind of dump him here, but there's no way he can stay at the shelter." The nurse grimaces as I speak, clearly irritated that I've brought Oscar to Harborview, and she asks me if I'm going to stay with Oscar while he waits to be called. Before I can answer I hear a woman yell, "My son!" behind me, words she repeatedly yells as she approaches the triage station. When she arrives at the station she screams, "My son's been shot! He's been shot! Is he dead?! I need to know if he's dead!" at which point she seems to hop from foot to foot. She's utterly hysterical and is oblivious to the looks of everyone around her, so entrenched is she in her anxiety and fear. I feel bludgeoned by the moment's beauty and I wonder when I last observed such purity of expression and find that I'm unable to answer the question. "Goddamnit, is he *dead?!*" says the woman as she still manically hops from foot to foot, and one of the nurses at the station meanwhile tries to escort her out of the ER. "It's like that Denis Johnson story," I mutter, at which point my triage nurse asks me again if I'll be staying with Oscar and I tell her, "Unfortunately, I have to go back to the shelter." She projects irritation which prompts me to apologize for leaving but before I do I ask her, "Do you have stuff like that happen here a lot?" She looks at me impassively and then yells out "Next!" to the broken person behind me, but before I walk away she says, "We see it all. We're the last stop. Nothing escapes us."

I wake from a dream where I've died and now I'm panicked and panting and it's only with difficulty that I don't shake Peyton awake. It's 1 in the morning and I'm scheduled to get surgery in five hours, the reality of which fact I find to be absolutely terrifying. I'm being operated on today because an MRI determined that I have gallstones, gallstones that cause cramping episodes that incapacitate me completely. I often vomit during the episodes—which typically last thirty to forty minutes— and enter the fetal position while I wait for the cramping to end. In the months preceding the surgery I've sought to determine what the precipitants could be for the cramping episodes but frustratingly I've been unable to do so. I've also researched naturopathic cures—the most notable of which is apple cider vinegar—but the doctor I consulted insisted that surgery was the only viable option. Presently I'm lying supine on the mattress and I'm wide-eyed and paranoid and I'm unsuccessfully attempting to remember my dream. All I remember is that I died. I don't know whether my death was the result of murder or suicide or etc., only that in the dream I died and that at the moment of death I awoke. I worry the dream is premonitory and that there's going to be an anesthesia mishap, the result of which mishap being that

I die at the age of thirty-two. I feel lonely and scared and unable to accept the seeming inevitability of my impending death and consequently against my better judgment I shake Peyton awake. She rolls over and looks at me and without me saying a word asks me if I'm afraid which is a safe assumption given how much I've recently perseverated on the possibility of an anesthesia mishap. Peyton says, "What are you most afraid of?" and I tell her, "That I'm going to die during the surgery," and inexplicably Peyton shakes her head. She says, "I don't think that's it," and I ask her what she means, after which she stays quiet for fifteen or twenty seconds. She then says, "You know, if you were to die, Michael, I would never forget you. I would always honor you and cherish the time together that we had." I'm stupefied by Peyton's comment, as it seems to cut through all my levels of fear and denial, and still saying nothing tears start to stream out of my eyes. She says, "I would move on, but I wouldn't forget you. You would always be in my heart. So even if you die, Michael, in the end it'll be okay." "Thank you, honey," I say, at which point I kiss Peyton and then roll over, as I feel the need to cry but to do so alone. "I don't want to be seen," I think to myself, not even by the woman that I love. It would be too much for me. And too bright. That light would be too bright.

A local venue, Chop Suey, is having a soul night and I go there to pick up women which I make progress toward when I run into the roommate of my ex-girlfriend, Mackenzie. The roommate, Hayley, has an outfit that's non-existent and when I arrive in her vicinity she erupts like she's run into a celebrity. She yells, "Michael, I was waiting for you!" though there was no way she could know I was coming to Chop Suey, as I came on a whim because I was feeling libidinous. We hug each other and the hug lingers and soon the two of us begin to dance, the end result of which is that I put my arms around Hayley and squeeze her bountiful ass. An hour later we're at the apartment Hayley used to share with Mackenzie, the familiar sight of which apartment both unnerves me and stimulates me. We start to make out and then take off our clothes and at one point Hayley pulls away and says, "Did you ever think about me when you were with Mackenzie?" Hayley says this shyly, almost like a child, as if she's ashamed by her need to ask the question but nevertheless is determined to find out what the answer is. I say, "I thought about you all the time," and feel myself get an erection after I say this and meanwhile I'm sickened by how titillating I find betrayal to be. The truth is: I've lied. While I dated Mackenzie I didn't really think of Hayley sexually but at the moment I'm willing to say anything to fan the flames of my desire. I then say, "What about you? Did you think about me? When I was with Mackenzie, did you fantasize about us together?" to which Hayley says, "Of course not. I'm a good person. I have principles."

"You can't bring any mushrooms back," my sister says as we're at a train station in Amsterdam and at first I don't understand what she means. I say, "You mean because they're illegal in Germany?" after which my sister shakes her head and says, "No, because Mom made me promise to not let you bring any back." I roll my eyes at my sister's comment but she crosses her arms in consternation and then says, "Seriously. I'm not letting you bring the mushrooms back to Mom and Dad's." I say, "But I paid good money for these, Annie. I don't want to just toss them," which prompts my sister to shrug her shoulders and say, "You either toss them or take them right now." Impulsively I decide to take the entirety of the amount that I've purchased—which amounts to more than an eighth of an ounce of liberty caps—which I do here at the train station half an hour before boarding the train. The mushrooms come on ten minutes later and I feel an enormous upwelling of anxiety and I then tell my sister I've made a tremendous mistake. She says, "There's nothing you can do. Just ride it out, Michael. You have no control over the situation at all." This strikes me as profound and subsequently I become very quiet and soon thereafter I board the train and take my seat next to a window. I then proceed to stare out of the window and listen to Aphex Twin's *Selected Ambient Works 85-92* on repeat and for two hours feel like I'm on the cusp of something beautiful. I mutter, "The cusp of beauty is what's truly beautiful," and my sister looks at me like I'm an alien and then looks around us to see if anyone's heard what I've said. "Be quiet, and don't be weird," she says and this time I'm unsure if she's saying something insightful although she probably is and namelessness is what we should all aspire to.

Bill is suffering from alcohol withdrawal at my apartment which includes first shaking and then vomiting when I decide to try to make inroads into getting the man sober. I say, "We're both cokeheads, obviously. And in the long run that will kill us. But look at yourself, man: you're so addicted to booze that you're having DTs." Bill waves away the comment after puking and says, "Dude, you have to get me some beer. Otherwise this is going to last like twenty-four hours." I consider the merits of the comment and ultimately decide that he's right because if I refuse the request he could potentially die of a seizure. Am I enabling the man by getting him booze? The answer to that is obviously yes but it's also incredibly obvious that I'm not equipped to usher my friend through alcohol withdrawal. I walk to a nearby Plaid Pantry and purchase a six-pack of PBR and an hour later Bill seems to be at baseline. Nevertheless the experience was alarming and I tell the man as much before I ask him why he continues to drink. He says, "Without booze and coke I have nothing," and I'm not sure what he means, but what I do know is that ten years from now I think my best friend will be dead. "That's not true," I say, but tellingly I don't elaborate upon the comment because the truth is that even with drugs neither of us can be said to own a single fucking thing.

It's sesshin at the Zen center which means that every day for the past six days I've meditated seven hours and not spoken to anyone. Far from being relaxing the meditation has been utterly excruciating which is inevitable given the physical position I'm usually in. The pain is concentrated in my knees and as I sit it ceaselessly throbs and nothing touches it, not even high doses of NSAIDs. During the moments I'm not in pain I have all manner of grotesquerie flit through my brain, including sex fantasies, revenge fantasies, memories of mistakes that I've made, and visions of an armed gunman coming into the zendo and killing everyone present. I eat mindfully, and clean mindfully, and shit mindfully, and etc., and consequently my mind at all times feels almost unbearably lucid. Right now I'm alone on a walk during a period of unstructured time when it occurs to me that I haven't thought about being brain-damaged for at least forty-eight hours. In other words the narrative I've been feeding myself—that I've done permanent brain damage as a result of my use of psychedelics—is revealed to me to be one hundred percent false. Or if not false then the last two days have at least demonstrated to me that whatever brain damage I have is made exponentially worse by me telling myself that I'm brain damaged. "I am what I think," I say to myself and instantly I recoil at what I've said, as it strikes me as a little too close to Law of Attraction-type thinking. Still nevertheless however unsavory the association to the Law of Attraction is it's true that my mind is a powerful tool that doesn't need to turn against itself. However as I approach the zendo for more zazen I forget about my realization and think, "And now for another hour and a half of pain." It's only as I pass through the doorway of the zendo and after I bow to the zendo's buddha statue that I realize that even this last thought is an example of me making my own reality. "I'm at war with myself," I think as I seat myself on my meditation cushion, and it's true that I'm fighting a demon that hates me and won't rest until I'm dead. I think, "But you're not dead. So fight," and this strikes me as an excellent motivator, at which point I ignore the pain in my mind for the excruciating pain in my knees.

Yearbooks have been passed out and it's now that especially daunting period when you ask other students to write a message inside of yours. I get the usual drivel—

"You rock, Keen!" "Have a good summer!" etc.—but when at day's end I peruse my yearbook I'm baffled by one of the comments. It says, "White Power, Bitch!" and predictably lacks attribution, although based on the penmanship I know it was written by my friend, Eric. The following day I ask Eric why he wrote what he wrote and he says, "Because it's funny. And because we should be proud of who we are." I slowly nod after Eric's comment in an attempt to feign understanding but the truth is I'm confused and disgusted by the comment. I then say, "Proud of who we are? Who's 'we'? And what do we have to be proud of?" Eric looks at me matter-of-factly and says, "White people. And because we run this shit, dawg."

I'm crouched over and so is my sister and we're outside of our apartment complex in Panama and I have a magnifying glass in my hand. It's summer and the sun is hot and we're bored out of our skulls which is why we're engaged in the activity we're engaged in. By activity I mean burning ants, a form of sadism I learned about from a boy in my third-grade class, Ricky, and one that I'm still skeptical will work. When earlier this morning I informed my mother about my plans to burn some ants she looked at me quizzically and said, "Michael, that's not very nice." Still she located the magnifying glass and wordlessly gave it to me and my sister and just now my sister and I located some ants next to some bushes. I use the magnifying glass and soon enough an ant has been burned alive and my sister is disquieted by the entire scene. She says, "This is gross. I'm leaving," at which point she walks back toward our apartment and for my part I stare at the magnifying glass in my hand. I then stare at a cluster of nearby ants and wonder whether I should kill them too, not because I want to but just so I can say that I did. "I can always lie," I say to myself but then tell myself that lying is wrong, that at all times it's important to be forthright and honest and true.

I've just completed my fifth step and my sponsor, George, asks me how I feel and after he does so I take inventory of my emotional state. I say, "I feel good, George. But, to be honest, I didn't tell you anything I haven't told someone before. Bill and I used to do coke and ask each other to say the worst things we've ever done." George nods at the comment but I can tell he's disappointed, as he's told me before that he got enormous relief when he did his own fifth step. He says, "I hear you, but I think there's a difference between confessing something when you're coked out of your mind compared to when you're vulnerable and sober." I agree with the man and he then says, "Is there anything else you need to get off your chest?" and though I can't think of anything I still feel like I'm holding something back. I want to grab George by the shoulders and shake him and scream, "I'm fucked up beyond all reckoning!" but I assume this isn't a normal part of the fifth step. So instead I smile and say, "I've said it all," but the truth is that I didn't and that I can't, because how do I tell someone I'm so broken that there's no way I can ever be healed? George says, "You'll get relief. I promise you that," and I find myself agreeing with the man completely, although after the fact it occurs to me that he was talking about step nine and in my own mind I was thinking about death.

I'm broke and unemployed and am only able to pay rent because I'm on unemployment and I spend most of my days writing trash fiction at coffee shops. In order to maintain my unemployment benefits I have to apply to three jobs per week which I do though I have no interest in obtaining a job. Consequently I apply for jobs that it would be impossible for me to get, including a job as a yoga teacher, a nurse, a mechanic, a plumber, an electrician, an actuary, and a brain surgeon. One day I'm randomly selected to come into an office and prove that I'm applying and when I do the employment specialist looks at me and says, "You're applying to be a yoga teacher?" I say, "I got burned out doing social work. I'm trying to branch out." The employment specialist shakes his head but encourages me to keep applying which I do until my benefits run out thirty weeks later. Throughout this entire period I'm unable to afford my psychiatric medications, most notably my antipsychotic, Abilify, which is extraordinarily effective. My psychiatrist recommends that I get Abilify from India or Pakistan or etc., and though I'm skeptical I go to the website of a Canadian pharmacy in order to obtain my meds. Presently I'm sitting at my kitchen table when one of my roommates, Neil, brings in today's mail, and says to me, "Looks like you got a package from Istanbul." I can sense he's intrigued and assumes I've ordered something illicit which from an American legal standpoint it's true that I have. "Drugs?" he says, at which point I nod my head and say, "Anything to escape the horrors of the human brain," to which Neil smiles and says, "I couldn't agree with you more."

It's my first college debate team meeting and I listen to the motivational speech given by the debate team captain, Charlie, and as I do so I mentally prepare for what I'm going to say. I was recruited the year before to be part of Berkeley's debate team which in fact is the primary reason—or so I'd guess—why I was granted admission to the university. "Recruited" is perhaps too strong a word as I simply spoke to Charlie after getting second place at the Berkeley high school tournament, a tournament where Charlie judged me and voted for me in the final round. In a sense debate saved me, as it gave me an activity through which I could channel my energy, an activity that was healthy and stimulating and that had nothing to do with drugs. I was also prodigiously good at it and in fact at the most prestigious tournament in the country—the Tournament of Champions, which is hard to even qualify for—I performed better than all but sixteen debaters. However near the end of my high school career I grew tired of debating as the activity seemed to inculcate a toxic mindset in everyone I knew. That is to say it prevented debaters from listening to people—genuinely listening, that is—and instead encouraged them to consider the flaws or deficiencies in whatever was being said. While useful as a skill I found that this tendency to focus on flaws was difficult to curb, even in those conversations where listening openly and compassionately was the goal. Having gone to the Zen center post-graduation and having seen the power silence and attention can have I've since decided to quit the debate team even though I've only just joined it. Charlie finishes his speech and encourages the debaters to break into clusters, this so that the new debaters can introduce themselves to the older members of the team. I approach Charlie straightaway and ask him if I can speak to him in private and seconds later we're standing outside of the debate team room. "I can't do this," I say. "If I debate, it'll be toxic for me." For his part Charlie looks confused by what I've said. He says, "What do you mean by 'toxic'? How is college debate in any way toxic?" I proceed to explain my position which is chiefly comprised of my conviction that I can't listen to people non-judgmentally if I participate in debate whatsoever. Charlie says, "I don't understand. Being judgmental is important. A lot of people say stupid things, and those people deserve to be judged." I say, "I don't want to live that way," to which Charlie says, "You're making a mistake," to which I shrug my shoulders and say, "I hear what you're saying."

I'm at my Sunday meeting in Capitol Hill where I've been a regular for over a year when my friend, Bobby Lee, is called on to share. Bobby Lee is voluble and quick to laugh and is also exceedingly friendly and most movingly he was the person who called me most consistently when I was in the midst of my relapse. In other words I have affection for the man and consider him to be a loyal and caring friend and if someone were to ask me I'd say he's one of the most honorable people I know. During his share Bobby Lee starts by riffing on the topic raised by the meeting's chair, Charmagne—the topic is the fourth step—and predictably he says insightful things about the importance of conducting a fearless and thorough moral inventory. Near the end of his share however he directly addresses the regulars among us in the meeting and says, "All of you guys know me as an upstanding man. The truth is: I am that man, but I'm not just that man. I'm also a registered sex offender who, while he was still in active use, did some very, very bad things. To the degree that I can I've made amends for those things, and in the here and now I try to make living amends by being a good person. The reason I bring it up is that if I let it, the guilt and shame could consume me. I could drink and drug myself to death because part of me thinks that's what I deserve. But through the help of my higher power, I've come to see that there's something worth salvaging with me. I've come to see I'm not worthless, I'm not broken, I'm not scum. I've made terrible mistakes, yes, but I'm also worth saving. I say all of this to take responsibility for what I've done, but also to show you that forgiveness is possible, that if you work the steps it's something that's entirely within your reach." With this Bobby Lee goes silent and Charmagne calls on the next person to share but as for me I sit stupefied by what I've heard. This man whom I love, whom I consider to be one of the most principled people I know, is currently on the sex offender registry? I'm floored by the revelation and have to shake my head at how little I understand other people and the world, at how complex everyone and everything around me really is. After the meeting I approach Bobby Lee and tell him his share was courageous and inspiring and he shakes my hand and thanks me for what I've said. I say, "I wish I could be like you. I have so much shame about my behavior. It feels like no matter what I do I'm not going to be able to escape it." Bobby Lee looks me over to appraise me and then says, "You might not ever escape it completely. But that's okay. Shame can keep you on the straight and narrow, and in so doing it can ensure that you follow the righteous path." I then say, "I'm grateful for you Bobby Lee. You're a good person, and you don't meet a lot of those," to which he says, "I raped a child. I'm not good. Let's not go crazy."

I'm in Manhattan eating lunch with Abe whom I haven't seen in close to a decade and in that period our life paths have radically diverged. Abe became a pilot after high school who flies charter planes around India and on one occasion even flew George Lucas around the country. Meanwhile for my part I went to college and then lived in Japan for a year and now I'm attending a master's program in social work at Columbia. We reminisce about the days of doing drugs—days evidently that we each have left behind—and about people from Puyallup, most of whom we've both completely lost touch with. Eventually the topic turns to my master's program and when it does Abe becomes bizarrely confrontational, sufficiently confrontational that he says, "There's no point in going to college. I make really good money being a pilot. I wouldn't go to college even if the government paid for all of it." Sensing an escalation in Abe's energy I attempt to defuse the situation, an attempt I make by saying, "Yeah, man. I get it. No need to waste money on college. You found your passion, and you followed it. And that's rad." He says, "College is dumb. It's fucking stupid. Just a bunch of rich assholes who want to say they've read *Moby Dick* or whatever. Like, who cares about that shit, you know what I mean?" Irritated I say, "*Moby Dick* is actually really good. There's a section called 'The Whiteness of the Whale' that's totally rad. And all the stuff with the captain, Ahab, is super, super good." Abe says nothing in response, focusing on his linguine, and in the silence I feel bad for lording my education over the man. I say, "But I get your basic point. College is useless. It's probably a waste that I'm doing it. I envy you being able to fly all around Asia." Abe wipes his lips off with his napkin and doesn't seem to acknowledge the olive branch. He then says, "'The Whiteness of the Whale'"? What, is the whale a neo-Nazi or something?"

I'm stoned and with Peyton and I've put my head onto her lap and she's brushing my hair with her hand as we talk about the future. Earlier today I proposed at a restaurant that we frequent on the weekends in Lafayette—Another Broken Egg—and the memory of getting down on one knee brings a smile to my face. Suddenly our sweet dullard of a puppy jumps onto the couch and begins to lick every part of my face which is to say his slobber stains my forehead, my cheeks, my lips, even my eyelids. The licking is overwhelming and I'm trapped and Peyton is laughing at how much I'm squirming as a result of the compulsive licking and I too am laughing at how absurd the situation is. The moment is wondrous and pure and I feel trapped in it in the most glorious way, by which I mean I'm lost in it, I mean completely and utterly lost. In other words I've completely lost my bearings and am floating along in the ether with these beings I love so much and I wish I could stay here with both of you forever. And of course I can in a sense I can call it to mind now today at this very moment and when I do it's all light and laughter and gratitude and hope so thank you.

I take a phone call from my mother who begins by saying, "Uncle Ryan is going to die in the next few hours," and my immediate response is to calmly ask, "What exactly is he going to die of?" My mother then informs me that my uncle is suffering from systemic organ failure, organ failure precipitated by alcohol abuse. "I knew his drinking was bad," my mother says. "But I had no idea it was bad enough to do this." My mother's voice is uninflected, as she's likely experiencing shock, and in the silence that ensues I think back on the last few years of my uncle's use. It was no secret that my uncle was drinking—this after years of being a member of AA—although evidently he did take steps to conceal how much he drank from my mother and father. I walk outside of my apartment during the phone call and kick pebbles in the parking lot and eventually I tell my mother that I'm going to call my aunt to see if there's anything I can do. I then call my aunt Ruth and she answers the phone within one ring and after she does so she says, "Uncle Ryan just died. I have to go." My aunt then ends the call, at which point I call my mother to inform her of her brother's death, and when I tell her she starts crying on the phone. Eventually my mother reins in her tears and says, "At least the kids and Ruth will be okay. The life insurance policy at Boeing is probably good." I'll learn in the coming weeks that my aunt's going to receive something like a million dollars, a sum that I assume will help my two cousins go to college. Eighteen months after my uncle's death the entire million dollars will be gone, as my aunt will have started using meth in the immediate aftermath of her husband's death. Evidently in her manic and psychotic state my aunt is unbelievably reckless with her money, buying cars and drugs and etc. for all manner of ne'er-do-wells in the city of Kent. In the decade following my uncle's death I have minimal contact with my cousins and no contact whatsoever with my aunt Ruth. I meet with one of my cousins, Lucas, and his wife and I gingerly bring up the topic of my aunt and when I do Lucas looks at his hands. He says, "We don't talk. I love her though. And I hope she knows I forgive her for all the money stuff," and when he says this his wife kisses him on the cheek. I say, "I'm glad you both have each other," at which point Lucas looks at his wife and says, "Life is unbearable if you don't have love," and after which I modify Lucas's words by saying, "You're right, Lucas: life is unbearable."

My mother calls me and is crying and tells me that my father is ranting about black culture, etc., and that whenever she calls him out he screams at her and calls her a cunt. I'm at a loss for how to respond because I want to offer emotional support to my mother but I also know that it's vital that I keep my nuclear family at arm's length. My father is tyrannical and abusive and contaminates everything within his reach which is to say that if I get ensnared in his bullshit I'll be drained by him as if he were an emotional vampire. "I just don't know what to do," my mother says. "This isn't the man that I married." I suppress the impulse to check my mother because the truth is that my father today is the man he's always been and I've been telling her since I was five that she should get a divorce. In other words I have anger toward my mother for choosing to never leave my father, this though she's had many opportunities to do so over the course of my life. She repeats, "I just don't know what to do," and it's clear to me that she's seeking some form of reassurance, reassurance that I'm unable to offer because she's hitched her wagon to a man who is basically a monster. "It'll be okay, mom," I say. "Annie and I are here for you, you know?" at which point my mother begins to cry on the phone. I think to myself, "You made your bed, mom, so you have to lie in it," but decide not to share this because it's cruel, which I'm not immune to of course I'm just as sadistic as the next guy. Maybe even more so. I don't know.

My mother says, "What would it take for you to talk to your father?" and I tell her that there's nothing he can do, that I hate the man and will never speak to him again. I say, "Did you forget what he did the last time he saw me? He carried a hammer around the house and said he was going to bash my head in while I was sleeping," to which my mother says, "No one's perfect, Michael. Everyone makes mistakes." I cackle at the comment and am preparing to tell my mother that I want to change the subject when she unexpectedly plays the cancer card. She says, "I don't know how much time I have left, Michael. The cancer has metastasized, you know. For all I know I could be dead in six months." I say, "I know that, Mom. I know. But what does that have to do with me talking to Dad?" to which she says, "I don't want to die knowing that you two aren't on speaking terms." A silence ensues during which I feel an upwelling of guilt and before I respond my mother repeats her previous question. She says, "So is there anything he can do? Anything at all? If he apologizes for the hammer thing? He told me he's willing to apologize for that." I look at my bowl of oatmeal as she says this and briefly wonder what it would be like to live well above the poverty line—I live on a paltry stipend from my PhD program—and in an attempt at humor I say, "I'll talk to him if he gives me fifteen thousand dollars." My mother doesn't laugh which I take to mean my dad might accept the ludicrous condition that I've offered and this worries me because of course that means I'll have to speak to my dad. My mother says, "I'll talk to Dad," and soon thereafter she ends the call and five minutes later she calls back and says my father won't give me fifteen thousand but will give me ten. I feel my jaw drop and consider reneging on principle but in addition to needing the money there's something poetic about my dad having to pay me off. I say, "Fine. Ten thousand. But I'm not talking to him until the money is in my account," and within forty-eight hours I'm ten thousand dollars richer. I end up speaking to my father and the conversation is comically cold which is to say that two minutes into it he says, "I don't know what to talk about with my boy." Over the course of the next year my cocaine use devolves into clear addiction, to such a degree in fact that probably ninety percent of my father's money is spent on drugs. One night in late July 2021 I withdraw money from the ATM and see that I have less than five hundred dollars in my account. "He deserves it," I say as I head toward Zeke's and seconds later it occurs to me that I don't know who I'm speaking about, whether it's me or my father if there even is a difference between the two.

I'm in a car with my coworker, Natalie, and we're driving back to Sound Mental Health after completing an errand when I ask her if she's ever gotten close to dying. She says, "One time, yeah. I was probably doing eighty on the freeway. I hit some black ice, and my car started circling around and went across three lanes of traffic."

"Holy shit," I say. "Were you injured?" a question to which Natalie shakes her head. She says, "No. Not a scratch. I was incredibly lucky." I then say, "I'm curious. People say that your life flashes before your eyes at times like that. Did that happen to you? Did your life flash before your eyes?" Natalie says, "Not really, no. But what did happen is that I was flooded with regret. I thought about people I'd hurt, and things I wish I had done." "How interesting!" I say and at this point I'm ready to change the subject but before I can Natalie turns the tables on me. She says, "What would you regret if that happened to you?" at which point I ask for clarification on precisely what she means. She says, "If you were flooded with regret. What do you think your regrets would be?" and the thought that instantly occurs to me is that I would regret not trying to be an artist. "I'm not sure," I tell Natalie but the thought I've had is utterly overwhelming, to such a degree in fact that after work I tell my friend, Noah, that I want to apply to MFAs. The following fall I apply to fifteen programs and get rejected from every one, and the year after that I apply to fifteen more. I get waitlisted at one—Syracuse—and am eventually admitted, after learning which I run around my apartment screaming. Over the course of the next nine years I complete at least a novel-length work every six months which means that when I begin *Notes from the Trauma Party* I've completed approximately twenty novels. I query agents for ten of these and receive minimal interest in any of them and as I age out of my thirties I start to feel like a failure as a writer. Now I'm writing this section of *Notes from the Trauma Party* and I take a break to have a cigarette and as I smoke I tell myself,

"I've done what I said I would. I've spent the last decade trying to be an artist." I finish the cigarette and throw the filter in one of the shelter's garbage receptacles and as I reenter my office I smile and think, "You're a failure, Michael. But at least you fucking tried."

I'm on the phone with my mother and am poised to end the conversation when suddenly she tells me she's scared. "What of?" I ask her, expecting her to say something about cancer but instead she starts talking about the Mexican border. She says, "Biden's letting everyone in. Murderers. Rapists. You name it. We're close to the border, and I'm worried our city, Sahuarita, is about to get violent." I'm baffled by the comment—baffled and irritated, that is—and ask her what makes her think the town is going to be overrun with criminals. She says, "The government's doing it intentionally. They're sick of white people running the show. I don't know. I'm just scared, Michael. I'm scared." I want to excoriate my mother for her insanity but I detect real fear in her voice and so my primary objective is to provide comfort to the woman. I say, "I promise you, Mom: you have nothing to worry about," to which she says, "You're not safe, either, honey. For God's sake, you live in Seattle."

At the age of seventy my dad published a poetry collection and after he did so he quit writing entirely. I proofread the collection before it was published and even provided editorial feedback for my father, the latter of which netted me $150. During this editorial phase I told myself that I was only helping my father for the money but the truth is that I greatly admire my father's writing. I know it's not perfect—in fact it's often very flawed—but I like that in his poems it feels like there are always two warring emotional states. Love and hate. Anger and acceptance. Clarity and confusion. Etc. Even more, his poems sometimes possess a religious sensibility that I find to be moving. During this period—in the early 2010s—I think of one of my father's poems nearly every single day and certain lines seem to be emblazoned across my eyelids. As time wears on I think of my father's poems less and less until today on the phone I broach the topic of writing with my father. I say, "Do you ever write at all, Dad?" a question which my father answers in the negative, saying, "I don't give a shit. And to be honest I don't think I ever really did." I say, "But there's beauty in some of your poems. You don't think that that beauty matters?" I hear him laugh on the phone and he says, "Where has beauty ever gotten anybody, Michael."

I'm thirteen years old and I've been invited to hang out with the coolest kid in school, Frank, an invitation that once extended I immediately and joyfully accept. I live in Puyallup, Washington, a town whose only claim to fame is the Puyallup Fair, a fair in Washington whose fairgrounds are the location of a former Japanese internment camp, Camp Harmony. It's an unreal city, under the chrome sky of car dealerships and strip malls, and as an adult I'll joke about how out of all of my childhood traumas simply living in Puyallup was the biggest. It's a Saturday and early summer and it's sufficiently hot that everyone needs a cool place to be indoors which the South Hill Mall provides as does every other air-conditioned mall in America. Once I enter the mall I meet up with Frank at Tower Records, a store I either stole a CD from the year before or confabulated the memory that I did. We then each purchase an Orange Julius and are sipping away at them in the food court when Frank asks me to hand my Orange Julius over to him. I'm puzzled by the request and hesitate to hand it over when Frank suddenly zips open his backpack and flashes the label of a bottle of Southern Comfort. I give Frank my cup at which point he takes it to the restroom adjacent to the food court and replaces the sipped-up Julius with something like ten to twelve ounces of booze. It's the first time I've consumed booze or at least enough booze to get drunk and ten minutes of intermittent gagging later Frank asks for my cup. I'm proud to have finished my drink and I assume he's going to throw the cups away but no after he takes them Frank strolls back over to the restroom. When eventually he returns he theatrically swishes each cup in his hand which is meant to serve as an explanation for what he's done. Namely fill up the empty cups with water, water and an additional quantity of booze, booze that despite how drunk I am Frank seems intent on us consuming. Frank then says, "My parents are gone for the weekend. Let's take the bus back to my house." I sycophantically nod as I'm just grateful to be in Frank's presence and soon enough we're furtively drinking on the back of the bus that will drop us off close to Frank's house. Frank and I say nothing to each other on the ride over, each of us content to enjoy our own drunken thoughts, which in my case consist less of thoughts and more nervousness about entering Frank's home. We then exit the bus and arrive at his house which is very clearly the home of a family that's middle-class and before entering the home I take a moment to feel pity for Frank's parents. Frank has no brothers or sisters and based on what he's told me he's adopted which means in all likelihood that his adoptive parents are unable to have biological children. I push away my compassion when I enter the home and am immediately disappointed by how fastidiously clean the house appears, as I always envisioned Frank as semi-feral, not burdened by the usual trappings of suburbia. We lurch around his kitchen and eat chips and salsa and guacamole while disconcertingly Frank begins to look bored. Part of this I'm guessing is that by this point we're completely out of booze and part of it is that I'm still basically fawning over Frank. "I'm going to have some friends come over," Frank disinterestedly informs me and fifteen minutes later three additional people are standing in his kitchen. Two of the three are juniors, neither of whom appears at all interested in getting to know me, as evidenced by the fact that they don't shake my hand or in fact greet me in any way whatsoever. The third person, Bruce, is a thirty-eight-year-old man who supplies us with more booze, chiefly rotgut vodka and bourbon. Bruce, Frank, and the juniors talk while I contribute next to nothing and meanwhile I treat my social anxiety by drinking even more. Eventually Frank says, "I have something to show you all," at which point he herds us into his living room and asks us to situate ourselves on either a recliner, a chair, an ottoman, or a couch. Frank then puts on a VHS tape that depicts him talking to a girl I don't recognize and strangely enough the two of them on TV are in the same living room the five of us—Frank, Bruce, the juniors, and I—are in. "She didn't know she was being recorded," Frank says with a laugh, a laugh that's replicated by everyone else in the room. I can't hear what Frank and the girl are saying but in time I do observe the two taking off their clothes, after which point both begin to manually stimulate each other. I'm horrified by what I'm seeing but even more horrified by what my compatriots are doing which bluntly stated is that besides me every person in the living room is masturbating to the video of Frank and the girl now having penetrative sex. I feel myself dissociate or zone out or fully succumb to the feeling of drunkenness which is to say that irrespective of how it's conceived of I'm here in Frank's living room but not really in Frank's living room. "Why aren't you masturbating?" Frank eventually asks. "You not masturbating is making me feel weird." As a testament to my drunkenness or perhaps the extreme inappropriateness of what's occurring I answer Frank directly and seemingly fearlessly. I say "Because it is weird, Frank. This is making me really uncomfortable." I'm amnesic the next few minutes, having all but completely dissociated, and when others stand up—I'm uncertain whether anyone masturbated to completion—I return to reality and down the rest of my massively alcoholic drink. I then exit the recliner whereupon I feel an upwelling of nausea and observe my knees buckling to such a degree that I find I can't walk. At this point I collapse to the floor and vomit a staggering amount, the sight of which prompts Frank to yell, "Goddamnit, Keen!" Frank says, "Take Keen to my bedroom, Bruce. You can take care of him there." At this point that is today, July 3, 2022, I have questions about this particular moment, namely questions about what was going through Frank's mind. Did Frank want Bruce to punish me for not masturbating? Did Frank in fact know what was poised to occur? Or did Frank perhaps want me to endure what he himself had endured? I don't presently know nor in all likelihood will I ever but what I do know is that right now I'm being partially dragged down the hallway to a restroom. I proceed to vomit again only this time in the toilet, this while Bruce watches over me, tending to me like he actually cares about my well-being. And from a certain vantage perhaps he does. What I will say is that regardless of Bruce's motives or his moral nature or his own past personal trauma he escorts me to Frank's bedroom and assists me onto his bed. He gently takes off my shoes, untying the laces as opposed to just pulling them off, and then assists a near-comatose me in taking off my vomit-soiled clothing. And then, which is to say now, right now, at this exact moment in time, Bruce rapes me in the total darkness of Frank's bedroom. I say total darkness but there is a moment the door to the bedroom partially opens and though I've completely dissociated I see Nikki, an acquaintance of mine who hadn't yet arrived at Frank's when I entered the bedroom, haloed by the light of the hallway. She laughs and closes the door and the haloed image is seared onto my brain, it's seared and I latch onto it in order to escape the present. The present that is defined by that vile mixture of pleasure, shame, discomfort, self-loathing, anger, and fear, and oh right another helping of shame. When school resumes in the fall I'll have many people reference my experience with Bruce, many of these people tittering as they do so. Tellingly no one will inquire into my mental state or conceive of what occurred as a violation because I was thirteen, far too old—or so it would seem—to be understood as a victim. So strong is my trauma during this period that I dissociate whenever I even hear my rapist's name, a response that's so pronounced in fact that I can't even say how often this dissociative response occurs. I carry this shame and self-loathing and etc. until the age of eighteen, during which entire five-year period I discuss my rape with absolutely no one. Finally at eighteen at the Zen center I get stoned and tell two people I trust about the rape and the two, Bindu and Aaron, are incredibly supportive. Over the course of the next year I tell my friends and family about the rape and as at the Zen center everyone is incredibly supportive. I talk about the rape in therapy and feel less shame about what happened and am even capable when appropriate of telling people I don't know all that well about what happened. Progress is being made by which I mean I'm slowly becoming healed or so I tell myself until in a college class on sexuality I watch a video in a large auditorium on male sexual abuse. The words of the abuse victims strike a chord and the resonance is too much and I end up weeping in the middle of the crowded room. I also during this period frequently lose my erection during sex with women, by which I mean the slightest disruption in my concentration makes me dissociate during the sexual act. But still I'm making progress and the effects on my sexual psyche are becoming less catastrophic, this even though I still question my sexuality and can't tolerate digital penetration whatsoever. And then decades later which is to say now during the pandemic in 2020 I reconnect with Frank on Facebook. He's talkative and friendly and seems I think bizarrely interested in conversing and even on several occasions via Messenger tries to organize a time to get together. In other words his speech is charged and I'm positive contains some ulterior meaning and it's clear to me at that time that Frank wants to in some way debrief about that hideous night. And what's sad and pathetic and something I'm likely always going to regret is that I never take Frank up on his offer. No. I blow him off and deactivate Facebook and never broach the subject of my rape, nor do I ask him whether he was himself raped or haunted by guilt or etc. All of which is to say I don't receive an apology from Frank nor do I get any kind of closure whatsoever. Why? Because I'm a coward. And the unpleasant truth is this: I haven't fully healed from the trauma of the rape. I haven't forgiven all the players, I haven't accepted what occurred, or if I have it's only in my better and more spiritual moments. At my worst? At my worst I think of Frank and Bruce and the people who ridiculed me for being raped, I imagine them collectively opening Frank's bedroom door and being haloed like Nikki was by a nimbus of light. And right now—right *now*—to every last one of you standing in that doorway I say: you're not forgiven. And fuck all of you forever.

I just woke up from a dream and need to get this out as soon as possible because it's precious and will soon evaporate I can feel it. At the beginning of the dream I was sitting in a rocking chair and it was somehow clear to me that I'd aged a tremendous amount. Eighty, ninety, one hundred, all I know is that I was on the brink of death, I was in the chair and it was rocking of its own accord. I was also on a beach as I was steadily rocking back and forth and throughout the rocking I could feel the sand on my feet. I was rocking and it was noon and the sun was at its meridian or so I assume because I was looking out at the horizon and the sun was nowhere to be seen. No clouds, no rain, only blue never-ending blue but I could feel the sun beating down glory on my spindly arms and legs. Eventually I heard a voice a soft voice so soft I almost couldn't hear it and then suddenly I recognized the voice as belonging to Peyton. She was repeating the same word—"communion, communion, communion"—but I couldn't see Peyton I could only hear her voice. She was behind me somehow although I'm not sure how I knew that but the point is that I knew Peyton was speaking to me from somewhere behind me. I had the impulse to communicate to say something anything I don't know I had no idea what it would be but I wanted her to know that she had never left my mind. For some reason though I couldn't muster any form of speech which I remember thinking was strange until I heard a second voice emerge from somewhere behind me. It was Zoe's voice but I couldn't make out exactly what she was saying as her voice was competing with Peyton's which by this point had become very loud. Again I wanted to speak and again frustratingly I found that I couldn't until it occurred to me to turn around and make eye contact with Peyton and Zoe. What was deeply horrifying however was the realization that I couldn't turn around, that my body was both glued to and controlled by the rocking of the chair. The chair was rocking metronomically and I couldn't speak or move in any way and I was considering my predicament when I heard the voice of first my mother then my father and then etc. It was everyone in my life everyone over the course of my entire life their voices were part of the din and if I tried I could make out any given person. At this point in the dream I became reconciled to the idea that I would never be able to speak to or see the people behind me. The chair was rocking I couldn't stop it and all I could see was the horizon which was so blue I couldn't even distinguish it from the ocean below it. Everything was calm and I had resigned myself to this lack of control until I looked down at my body and realized I was no longer a human being. No. I was now a bee a bumblebee that was tied down to the chair by its abdomen and no matter what I did I couldn't escape the chair or its rocking. Obviously I couldn't talk as I didn't have a larynx or trachea or etc., but the point is that because I was a bee it was totally clear what had to happen. And what that was was this: I had to use my stinger that was my obvious destiny I had to sting something and in the process remove my stinger and abdomen. This frightened me initially—I didn't want to kill any other creature—until I looked down and saw my fleshy frame just out of reach of the rocking chair. By fleshy frame I mean my body the human body of Michael Keen which wasn't mine anymore as I was now a bee. Michael Keen's body was just out of reach and in an effort to reach this human body I began flapping my wings which altered the nature of the rocking. The base of the chair didn't move but the rocking motions got more pronounced until eventually my stinger penetrated the belly of my human body—which was standing, eyes closed and motionless, as if awaiting the fatal blow—at which point as the chair rocked backward my stinger and abdomen were ripped from me and remained in the body of Michael Keen. My bee-body began hemorrhaging blood and I knew I only had seconds to live which meant I had to escape the rocking chair to make eye contact with everyone around me. My wings lifted me out of the chair and I was poised to turn around yes I was preparing to look in the eyes of every last person who had affected my life.

And that's it. That's the dream. I woke up right as I was about to turn around. I wish I could say more. But I can't. I wish I could but I can't.

ABOUT THE AUTHOR

MICHAEL KEEN is from Puyallup, Washington, and has an MFA from Syracuse University. He also has an MSW from Columbia University, and has worked for many years as a social worker. *Notes from the Trauma Party* is his first book.

www.ingramcontent.com/pod-product-compliance
Lightning Source LLC
Chambersburg PA
CBHW031131130726
47988CB00006B/2321